Like the Patrick Melrose novels—but in miniature and in Maine—this wonderful and unusual novel-in-stories juxtaposes the downfall of the Howland family with the increasing disillusionment of one of its younger members, John. In laugh-out-loud prose, Jason Brown crucifies the esteemed Howlands, who consider themselves to be above all things (even life itself), as they struggle to understand their place in an increasingly unfamiliar world—one that is better for almost everyone *except* their family. What's waiting in the wings, then, for John? A needle in the arm or a place at the table of the anointed? *A Faithful but Melancholy Account of Several Barbarities Lately Committed* is a staggering portrait of inheritance and identity from one of our very best writers. ~ Marjorie Celona, *Y*

Jason Brown's *A Faithful but Melancholy Account of Several Barbarities Lately Committed* is, to say it simply, one of the best collections of linked stories I have ever read by anybody, at any time. One by one, these stories are riveting. When you finish the entire book, you will be shaking your head at their collective power. What a writer. What an artist. ~ Steve Yarbrough, *The Unmade World* and *The Realm of Last Chances*

How beautifully these linked stories lead us into a family history which is a thicket of old legends and superb characters. With its long span and its sharp views, this is a remarkable collection. ~ Joan Silber, *Improvement* and *Fools*

Jason Brown is a true master of the short story, and this book is wonderfully reminiscent of Elizabeth Strout's *Olive Kitteridge*. Tender and insightful, dotted with humor, these are stories of real human beings. Brown's characters are flawed and full of longing, aching for connection and haunted by history. Read this book. ~ Karen Thompson Walker, *The Dreamers*

With humor and wit, Jason Brown tells these delightful and true stories about New Englanders marinating in their history. These eccentric people indulge their desire to live outside of time. I love these stories in part for their mischievous exploration of the dangers of ignoring societal change. ~ Keith Scribner, *The Oregon Experiment* and *Old Newgate Road*

Calling to mind Salinger and O'Connor and Cheever, but with a dark vaudeville all its own, Jason Brown's *A Faithful but Melancholy Account of Several Barbarities Recently Committed* is thrilling. Ranging far and wide in time and place and character, these linked stories burrow deep into the history of a family and of a country, proving again that our shared past, though we may labor to ignore it, haunts us still. These are American stories at their finest. ~ Dan O'Brien, *The House in Scarsdale* and *New Life*

Jason Brown's Howland stories are marvels, all of them perfectly brined in centuries of heartbreak, privation, cruelty, yearning and self-delusion. This book is a brilliantly observed, emotionally risky and often quite funny reminder of what a linked collection can do. ~ Sam Lipsyte, *Hark* and *The Ask*

Like peeking through the windows of a family even more eccentric than your own. With each story, you find yourself sucked further into this coastal Maine community until you're damn near local. Masterful as it is playful, this is a serious look at the absurdity of family. ~ Mat Johnson, *Pym* and *Loving Day*

"In the mood for Maine? Let Jason Brown lead you through the remarkable generational trauma that inflicted (and continues to inflict) the Howlands. These ten accounts are surprising, moving, and wry. It's a pleasure to hold Brown's stories in your hands." ~ Rebecca Schiff, *The Bed Moved*

A Faithful but Melancholy Account of Several Barbarities Lately Committed

LINKED STORIES

Jason Brown

A Memorial of the present deplorable State of New-England . . . to which is added a faithful but melancholy account of several Barbarities lately committed upon Her Majesty's subjects.

—Cotton Mather, 1707, on Queen Anne's War

A Faithful but Melancholy Account of Several Barbarities Lately Committed

LINKED STORIES

Jason Brown

Missouri Review Books

Edited by Kristine Somerville and Speer Morgan

Missouri Review Books

Published by Missouri Review Books
357 McReynolds Hall, University of Missouri
Columbia, Missouri 65211

Missouri Review Books is published by *The Missouri Review* through the College of Arts & Science of the University of Missouri, with private contributions.

The following stories have been previously published: "Instructions to the Living from the Condition of the Dead," "The Last Voyage of the *Alice B Toklas*" and "Sarah Campbell's Story," in *The Missouri Review*; "The Last Voyage of the *Alice B Toklas*," also in the *Pushcart Prize Anthology 2020*; "Wintering Over," in the *Southern Review* and *Electric Literature*; "Return of the Native," in *Portland Monthly*; "Flood," in *Prairie Schooner*; "The Wreck of the *Ipswich Sparrow*," in *Dalhousie Review*; "A Faithful but Melancholy Account of Several Barbarities Lately Committed," in *Sewanee Review*; "Goat," in the *Bellevue Literary Review*; "Make Way For Ducklings," in *Washington Square Review*.

ISBN: 978-1-945829-24-6 (print)
ISBN: 978-1-945829-25-3 (digital)

Library of Congress Control Number: 2019944382

www.missourireview.com

Cover Image: *Raetur*, Alvaro Sanchez

Cover design by Jane Raese of Raese Design, Boulder, Colorado. Interior design by Scott McCullough.

For Nicola and Isabella

Table of Contents

The Howlands

John Howland (1591–1672) m. Elizabeth Tilley (1600–1687)
Plymouth Colony
Josiah Howland (1619–1683) m. Bridget Hutchinson (1618–1698)
Plymouth Colony/Cushnoc, Province of Maine
John Hosea Howland (1638–1730) m. Fear Coffin (1640–1720)
Head Tide/Howland Island, Province of Massachusetts Bay
John Howland (1676–1770) m. Experience Storrs (1699–1742)
Howland Island, Province of Massachusetts Bay
Robert Howland (1720–1780) m. Sarah Campbell (1722–1787)
Howland Island, MA
William Howland (1757– 1820) m. Constance Mainwaring (1752–1789)
Vaughn/Howland Island, MA
John Jacobs Howland (1780–1850) m. Elizabeth McDill Jacobs (1780–1864)
Vaughn/Howland Island, ME
John Mainwaring Howland (1816–1901) m. Hannah Boynton Cousins (1812–1844)
Vaughn/Howland Island, ME
John Boynton Howland (1837–1920) m. Mabel Ross (1850–1930)
Vaughn/Howland Island, ME
John Hayes Howland (1880–1961) m. Mary Devereux Fogg (1891–1955)
Vaughn/Howland Island, ME

CURRENT

John Stoughton Howland (1911–2008) m. Sarah Libby (1911–2000)
Vaughn/Howland Island, ME
(1) Henry Parsons Howland (1940–) m. Lucinda Nutting Withers (1946–)
Vaughn, ME
(daughter) Elizabeth Parsons Howland (1970–)
Chicago, IL
(son) Mainwaring Hayes Howland (1976–) m. Caroline Palfrey Adams (1976–)
(grandson) William Palfry Howland (1997–)
Ojai, CA
(2) John Libby Howland (1944–) m. Rebecca Clough (1942–)
Chiapas, Mexico
(son) John Jacobs Howland (1966–) m. Mary McKinney (1969)
Eugene, OR
(daughter) Bridget Hutchinson Howland (1968–) m. William Rollo St. Launceston (1958–)
New York, NY
(3) Alden Fogg Howland (1955–2013) m. Sandra Elizabeth Stevens (1955–)
Arrowsic, ME
(daughter) Anna Howland (1973–)
Arrowsic, ME

(son) Henry Howland (1979–)
Boston, MA
(4) John Carlton Howland (1946–) m. Hannah Robinson Wingate (1943–)
San Mateo, CA
(son) Andrew Cousins Howland (1970–)
Portland, OR
(daughter) Phoebe Hutchinson Howland (1969–) m. Michael Smith (1968–)
Palo Alto, CA
(grandson) Jacob Howland Smith (1989–)
Palo Alto, CA
(granddaughter) Natalie Hutchinson Smith (1993–)
Palo Alto, CA

Foreword

Five of the ten linked stories in *A Faithful but Melancholy Account of Several Barbarities Lately Committed* follow John Howland's comic struggle with his New England legacy. Over the course of the book, set on the Maine coast, where the Howland family has lived for almost four hundred years, we also follow John's grandfather, the elder John, his cousins Phoebe and Anna, and his grandmother Sarah.

The tradition of linked collections includes books that are united by place, character, or subject. James Joyce's *Dubliners*, for instance, is a collection formed around place and theme—Dublin, Ireland, Irishness, and the desire to escape paralysis. In Sherwood Anderson's *Winesburg, Ohio*, the journalist-flaneur George Willard is an observer but not the main character in many of the stories that capture the boiling, confined inner life of men and women living in a small Midwestern American town at the turn of the twentieth century. *Love Medicine* by Louise Erdrich is held together by several characters in different families on a Chippewa reservation in North Dakota and by the challenges of living as a Native American from the 1930s to the 1980s. It is among the more powerful examples of a novel-in-stories that focuses on conflicts within a community over an expanse of time. Linked collections such as Alice Munro's *The Beggar Maid* and Denis Johnson's *Jesus' Son* focus on the same main character in every story. They follow characters over a number of years and through a dramatic arc in a way that suggests a more traditional novel. Other books, such as Ernest Hemingway's *In Our Time* and Elizabeth Strout's *Olive Kitteridge*, place the same character at the center of half or more of the stories while allowing others to explore community, family, or the prominent themes in the book.

An advantage of such collections is their ability to deviate from the "tyranny of plot" that sometimes dominates a conventional novel. In a linked collection, the writer can take a left turn and introduce new characters late in the book. Characters experience insights and change in proportion to the stories, which relieves the writer of the burden of having to furnish an outsized character change or self-realization. The stories stand alone, yet they also contribute to a larger narrative arc that satisfies readers in the way that a conventional novel can.

One of the prominent themes of Jason Brown's collection is the slow and often comic crumbling of Protestant male culture as the epicenter of American life. The Howland family does not come from an urban power center, but like some of the families in Faulkner's novels and stories, they are highly conscious of their history as patriarchs isolated in the decaying trappings of the family's past. The grandfather, John Howland, lives in a fantasy that still places him at the center of the world. The next generation lives in the confused ruins of the 1960s rebellion, while many in the third generation—to which the young John Howland belongs—feel that they have no choice but to scatter in search of a new identity.

At the dawn of the twenty-first century, some of the women of the family discover a sense of identity that eludes the Howland men. The young John leaves the isolation of the Maine coast for the desert and the West Coast, where he is befuddled and self-destructive. In his own halting way, he tries to shed an inherited worldview, and by the end of the book the young John finally gains traction on a modest life in Oregon, where blessedly no one cares about New England. When he returns to Maine for his uncle's funeral, we see that he resists the old ways of thinking, yet as the story progresses he cannot entirely shed the way he was raised, as no one does.

In the final story, "Sarah Campbell's Story," we go all the way back to the beginning of the Howlands' history in Maine to witness the incredible struggle that many faced as they traveled to the fledgling "immigrant nation." We also see the central role that religion played in forming a narrative about survival and the striving for dominance in the New World. Like the tales of Nathaniel Hawthorne, Brown's stories track the cultural and psychological evolution of New England puritanism while capturing the lingering burden that remains.

In his 1938 book *Maule's Curse: Seven Studies in the History of American Obscurantism*, Ivor Winters wrote one of the earliest attempts to integrate the Puritan ways of thinking into the history of American literature. "The puritan view of life was allegorical. . . . The puritan theology rested primarily upon the doctrine of predestination and the inefficaciousness of good works; it separated men sharply and certainly into two groups, the saved and the damned, and, technically, at least, was not concerned with any subtler shadings" or with what Winters calls "the chaos . . . of actuality." In the background of Brown's stories, we glimpse some of the chaos of early New England and of the true barbarities committed by the Howlands and those like them in the name of conquest and colonialism.

Speaking of the early puritans and their descendants, Winters says, "The imperceptive, unwavering brutality of many of the actions committed in the name of piety in the Massachusetts colonies more than justified the curse and prophecy by Mathew Maule from Nathaniel Hawthorne's *The House of the Seven Gables*, that God would give these Puritans blood to drink; in the name of God, they had violently cut themselves off from human nature; in the end, that is in Hawthorne's generation and in generations following, more than one of them drank his own heart's blood." Living more than a century after Nathaniel Hawthorne wrote his allegories of New England puritanism, some members of the Howland family in *A Faithful but Melancholy Account of Several Barbarities*

Lately Committed strive to rejoin the world their ancestors condemned. But whether they stay at home where they were born or relocate across the country, all members of the family discover that the past awaits them. "Nothing remembered, nothing forgotten."

KS & SM

Instructions to the Living from the Condition of the Dead

(2003)

John Stoughton Howland,
William Palfry Howland

The door hinges creaked, and the thudding footfalls of his family shook the beams. What were they doing here today, the day before Thanksgiving? Voices downstairs, the crackling of grocery bags, firewood clunking in front of the hearth—because they thought he was too old now to carry it from the barn himself. They swarmed into every corner of the parlor and the kitchen with no thought to the most important question, the same this year as every year: who had brought the goddamned cheddar? Two years ago he'd put his foot down and said he would no longer provide. So this year would be the same as last year: crackers and hummus.

"Dad? Where are you?" called Caroline, his grandson's mealy-mouthed wife, a doctor who talked tough about the importance in old age of regular bowel movements. A sharp slap on the staircase, then another and another. Nowhere to retreat to except his bedroom. Not safe! The first place they would look. The bathroom, and once there, into the cast-iron tub. Forced to evacuate because these people had showed up on Isabel's birthday. His family didn't even know about Isabel and wouldn't approve if they did. Their beloved Grandma Sarah departed, and here he was sneaking over to Isabel's house. Tut-tut, the old Heathcliff. No cheddar for him!

The slapping grew louder as he decided to stand his ground on the other side of the bathroom door (they had just once, he and Isabel, lain side by side in her great bed, with their clothes on, and he had leaned over to kiss her). "Your wife was very pretty," Isabel said. "She is," he replied, and this would've been a good chance to explain—though he decided it was not wise—the overwhelming feeling that his wife was not dead but everywhere around him at all times.

He heard no sound for almost a minute, so he opened the door to the bathroom. Five small fingers rested on the top step. The scruffy blond hair. The blue eyes and tanned face of his great-grandson, William Palfry Howland (Will), resident of Ojai, California. Having summited the top step, his great-grandson sighed.

"Daddy wants to talk to you," he said and cocked his head.

"The grand one or the regular one?" John asked.

He heard his wife, Sarah, clucking in the air around him. She didn't need to tell him to leave the boy be.

His great-grandson frowned and pursed his lips. The smallness of his mouth reminded John of Caroline, the boy's mother, who measured her words like a butcher adding slices of roast beef on the scale. The more she spoke, the more he would have to pay.

"Ah, I don't know what dayyy wants," Will said and shrugged. Cocking his hip and raising his hand in the air, Will flashed that sly smile, head tilted.

"Do you want to play a game?" John asked.

"No." Will shook his head.

"Well, you're in luck because I have a secret stash of cookies. . . ."

"Why?"

"Why? So no one else will eat them."

This seemed to cause horrible confusion. Will put his palm up to the side of his head.

"I don't like cookies," Will said.

"Everyone likes cookies," John countered.

"Do they have sugar in them?"

"Do they have sugar? Of course. They're cookies."

Will shook his head sadly. As always, John had lost the battle before it even started.

"What the heck do you like to eat, then?"

"Mangoes. I like mangoes."

"Would you like to do something for me?" He was out of tricks.

"Yes, I would!" The blue of Will's eyes seemed to deepen around his pupils.

"Go downstairs and tell your dad and your granddad—tell anyone you see—that you spotted me down by the river in back of the house."

"But you're not down by the river."

John knelt in front of Will's face.

"That's the point of the game, Will. If I were down by the river, it wouldn't be a game at all. Don't you see?"

"No." He shook his head. "I don't see."

"Well, you will someday. Now hurry up before it's too god-damned late."

"You swore," Will pointed out, but he didn't seem upset about it. He descended the steps carefully and, with a good deal less urgency than John would've liked, turned the corner to tell every-one that he had spotted his great-grandfather headed for the shore. John heard the side door slam. Everyone spilled out into the field behind the house and started calling his name.

Even on days when he managed a decent bowel movement, the narrow staircase was an iffy proposition (not recommended by Doctor Pingree or Janine, the attractive acupuncture woman, without whom he would not have a bowel movement). He grabbed his volume of Emily Dickinson, creaked down the stairs, stutter-stepped to the landing, plucked his Irish tweed hat off the hook, and headed out the front door to his electric tricycle parked at the head of the drive. Didn't need the motor going downhill. He slipped past the cars at the end of the drive, banged a left, and coasted toward Boynton's Market. Couldn't show up without a cupcake. She was only eighty-five—a younger woman. Flowers, too much. She always had flowers, anyway. How did she manage that in the winter? They hadn't even taken away her license yet, so maybe she drove to Portland for them. A girl with a license. They'd taken his away, even though he could see an osprey pluck a mole out of the grass at a hundred yards. He pedaled along the flat on Water Street and rode up onto the curb in front of Boynton's Market. Charlie Boynton manned the counter today.

"John," he said in his usual flat voice. Anchored there for twenty-five years.

"Gotta house full of people," John said.

"Happens this time of year."

"They weren't supposed to come 'til tomorrow. Charlie, I need a cupcake. A large cupcake if you have one. Two. Do you even have cupcakes today?"

"We have cupcakes."

Thank God, and tremendous cupcakes they were. He bought one carrot with thick cream frosting and one double chocolate. Charlie fit them up with a box, no great shakes, tied with string, just right for Isabel. A no-nonsense Holyoke girl, weren't many of them around, and two books of poems to her name. Isabel Vaughn Bowditch, though everyone called her Bella Vaughn, because she was a Vaughn first, especially as far as the town was concerned. The last Vaughn still living in Vaughn. Trim and strong in her

4

yellow slicker and Wellies, drove the old Volvo to the post office for the mail at exactly 10:45 every single morning. Her grandfather would've been Henry Vaughn, the one who ran the mill into the ground. Not his fault. Her brother the one who turned it into a retirement center. Her husband, Walter Bowditch, bald as a harbor seal, dead five years now, a "fancy mechanic," wanted to be a specialist in Portland, people said, but Bella said no, so he stayed in Vaughn and dispensed pills and cough syrup.

His own wife, Sarah, grew weak around the ankles in her last years. John did the shopping and cooking and cleaning. Then one morning he woke with the light as usual, swung his legs out of bed as he shivered in the cold bite of the bedroom air, and said, as he always did, "Going to take the dog out." Instead of saying "Okay" in her perfectly clear voice (she always woke before him and lay in bed waiting for the sun to come up), she said nothing. Made no sound. She lay on her back, mouth open, eyes closed.

Unsure that the half-charged tricycle battery would power him up the hill, he pedaled as far as he could before hitting the power switch and letting the motor take over. If he could make the next rise, he could coast the rest of the way past the Small and Nason places to reach Isabel's driveway. She'd told him when he last visited . . . ten days ago? Said he shouldn't worry about her birthday.

The motor on his trike started to whine a hundred yards from the crest of the hill. He pressed down hard on the pedals and, in the final stretch, stood up as sweat pooled on his brow. Over the top, he ran before the wind down the other side.

"For me, all that business with the body is over now," Sarah's voice entered his ear. "Go to her if that's what you want." Sometimes she spoke from above, high in the clouds, or from across the room.

He did want to smell Isabel's hair and rest his lips on the nape of her neck. He wanted to pull her to him.

"What if I lose track of you?" he said to his wife.

"You won't," she said.

He glided past the Tetherly house, the Wells house (someone from New York lived there now), the Coffin house with the windows shamefully fallen out of the cupola. The same was true of the Dill house, where Betsy had lived alone since her husband, Henry Dill, owner for forty years of Foot Wise Shoes in Augusta and active member of the volunteer fire department, had stepped in front of the snowplow, either on purpose or not, according to what you believed. Having only recently sold the store, he had talked to John about buying an electric tricycle for himself (one, he thought, with a stronger battery). No person who wanted to own an electric tricycle could possibly want to throw himself in front of a plow, but, as Sarah had pointed out more than once, why was the man out on Water Street at twelve midnight on a Thursday during a snowstorm? No one would ever know the answer to that question.

Second Street swept down to level ground. The sky began to clear, and the air, tinged with woodsmoke, turned sharp in his sinuses and hard as a fist in his chest. The body mechanic Pingree had said he had emphysema years ago, yet he felt it was only yesterday when he first stepped up to Sarah's parents' house and asked to see their daughter. "No, you may not!" It was a Sunday, the father reminded the young man. No piece of information had ever seemed as trivial and funny as the day of the week. He told her father he'd come back the next day, the eighth day of the week. "There is no eighth day," the father said, clearly baffled. "There is now," John told him.

And there was, and there is, still.

He slipped into Isabel's driveway. When the ground grew too rough and the ruts too deep, he stepped off the trike. Eager to reach the front door, he forgot the box of cupcakes and had to turn back.

"You should've brought flowers," Sarah said.

"She has flowers already," he said.

"But that's not the point."

He knew she was right, and he stood in front of the door wondering if he should turn back to Boynton's. For the last two months he'd called Isabel before sleep each night, and they read

Emily Dickinson to each other as they both gazed out their bedroom windows at the moon hanging over the twisting current of the river.

> *I had been hungry all the years;*
> *My noon had come, to dine;*
> *I, trembling, drew the table near,*
> *And touched the curious wine. . . .*

After more than sixty years of marriage and almost a century on earth, he could now feel himself pushing against the front of his pants like a schoolboy. He wanted to touch Isabel today, before the sun went down, before his family realized he'd abdicated his post the day before Thanksgiving (who would cut the turkey, light the plum pudding, start them off singing *We gather together to ask the Lord's blessing . . . ?)*

He pounded the brass knocker and listened with his ear to the door. For a moment, when he heard nothing, he stopped breathing. Then the house creaked under her light step. Those old pine floors with loosened rosehead nails, the horsehair plaster itself as alive as the hide of an animal.

"You would have been better off with her, John," Sarah said, and he shook his head. His father had said more or less the same thing when he first brought Sarah home: "Are you sure, John?" But what had John done with his life? A schoolteacher, correcting the spelling of the town. Sarah had risen to rule the school board. He hadn't deserved *her.*

The knob turned, and the door swung open. There she stood, trim in her white blouse and gray bob, a cup of coffee poised in her right hand. Her eyes jumped away from him, slid off his shoulder, and came to rest on the granite step. He didn't understand; there was no reason for her to be embarrassed. They'd done nothing that they couldn't take back. He could explain; he just wanted to come in, to not be outside.

"John," she said, and his patience gave out.

"Please, can I come in?"

"Of course." She bowed slightly and stepped out of his way, and he entered the foyer and the cool parlor. The threadbare oriental, the portrait of her grandfather, old Henry Vaughn, his chin like a rifle butt. He set the box on the sideboard and started to undo the string. She'd understand when he showed her the cupcakes. He struggled with the tape on the edge of the box and finally took out both cupcakes and placed them on the sideboard. The sight of them seemed to make her sad. He knew she liked chocolate.

"For your birthday," he said. How could anything be simpler than that?

"Today," she said slowly, "is not my birthday, John. It's next week."

Next week! He looked from the cupcakes to her. He'd spent so many afternoons looking right into her green eyes. She smiled out the window toward the brown straw of the field. At the end of the field, the barn, and beyond the barn a scattered veil of pines partially obscuring the river.

"I was going to call today and invite you to supper next week," she said.

He took *The Collected Poems of Emily Dickinson* out of his pocket and rested it next to the cupcakes.

She smiled and carried the cupcakes to the kitchen table. She would be right back. When she returned from the pantry, she carried a bottle of wine, her last bottle of Bocksbeutel, she said, from a case she and her husband had brought back from a trip to France and Germany in the late 1980s. He hadn't seen one of the distinctively round bottles of the Franconian wines in more than fifty years. She pulled the cork and filled two glasses. He toasted her upcoming birthday, and they both drank.

He lifted the book he had brought and was about to open to the poem "Hunger" when she sighed and told him that her favorite town in the wine region had been Tegernsee, and he set the book down on the table.

"Tegernsee?" he said, and she nodded. He asked if the wine in front of him came from this town. She nodded and lifted the bottle to pour him more.

"It was such a beautiful village, with those old hotels right on the lake and the mountains in the distance." She leaned forward, still smiling.

"We almost destroyed Tegernsee," he said.

"What do you mean?"

"It was the war," he said. He had told her he had been in the war, but they had never spoken of what he'd seen.

"Yes, of course," she said. "I didn't know there was a battle there. When we visited, the residents said none of the buildings had been destroyed. That there hadn't really been any fighting there."

She was right. His company commander, Bill Spears, spared the village because of a man named Heinz Shaeffer, a wounded German tank commander who walked toward them across a field with a bandage around his head and his one good arm raised in the air.

John had never spoken to anyone about the end of the war, not even to Sarah. Now as he talked, he began to search, like a man in a dark room, for an excuse to shut his mouth.

"We were chasing an SS unit down from Munich. They stopped in Tegernsee and started to shell us. So my commander told me to get on the phone and call for artillery. It was May 3. I was the forward observer—or that's what I had become after the other two were killed—so it was my job to calculate the coordinates.

"But then this man, a tank commander, walked out of the village.

"He told us the village was full of twelve thousand unarmed German soldiers, who were not SS, and war refugees and that the war would be over in days, and he was right—we knew that. The war ended five days later."

"So then it was a good thing you didn't destroy the village," she said, still smiling.

"But the armed SS unit was there, too, and they would get away down the back end of the valley into Austria. We didn't want to let them escape."

"But the war was almost over," she said and leaned forward to lay her hand on his forearm.

"We didn't care. We planned to execute every last one of them," he said.

"I don't understand. Why would you kill them if you knew the war was about to end?"

"Not kill—execute. Two different things. Because of the god-damned mess we found at Gardelegen and Kaufering, that's why." She tilted her head and squinted at him, and he lowered his voice. "Because of what we found."

"Oh, I see," she said and leaned back in her chair, the after-noon light turning to liquid in the reflections of her eyes. The corners of her mouth tucked in like the wings of a bird folding against its body. "Come, now," she said.

The words might have come from his own thoughts—he couldn't be sure—and he spoke to argue with himself.

"A thousand burned bodies inside one barn in Gardelegen," he said, "and that was nothing compared to Kaufering and Dachau . . . and all along the roadside to Tegernsee."

"Dachau?" Isabel shook her head with her eyes closed. "No, John," she said.

"I'm sorry," he said. "I shouldn't be telling you this." After they'd failed to attack Tegernsee, he and the others in his unit had never talked about what they'd seen.

"It's nonsense, John," she said, and she placed her hand back on his arm. He looked at her hand, at the Dickinson, at the cupcakes, then at the walls of the kitchen with pictures of her family: her late husband, her only child, Katherine, who lived in Boston, and other Vaughns, most of them gone now, the descendants of people who had, along with his own ancestors, started this town.

"But I was there," he said quietly, not to her exactly, and now he was forced to picture the man who had wedged his head under the wall of the barn and died with his eyes open to the sky. Had he seen that? The others they found in smoldering piles by the doors. Following the trail of the destruction south, they found more charred bodies inside the barracks at Kaufering. Skeletons with blackened skin stretched as tight as the heads of snare drums. Between Dachau and Tegernsee, more bodies in the woods and along the side of the road. Then they reached Tegernsee, and the tank commander with the bandage over one eye and another around his chest begged them not to shell the town where the murderers hid among the innocent.

"The SS is still there," John said to the CO, Bill Spears.

"And a hospital and twelve thousand people without guns," said the tank commander in perfect English. Dried blood flaked off his dirty neck. John remembered the German tank commander's hazel eyes, the chip in his tooth, the feel of the air, the impossibly blue sky as John held the handle of the radio in one hand and the crank in the other. Bill Spears raised his palm and shook his head. Later, they walked into the town with the tank commander. The SS had left already, and thousands of people, many of them children, mothers, grandmothers, wounded soldiers, all the people they would have killed, came out to greet them. Many people were dying in these last days of the war, Germans and prisoners both. Hundreds of thousands in the camps died of typhus before and after they were rescued. Many German villagers not killed by the constant Allied firebombing committed suicide just before the Americans or Soviets arrived.

"I know," Isabel said, "we are all supposed to think . . . Walter and I, we just never believed any of that—at least not in the way we were told it happened."

He realized she meant Kaufering, Dachau, and the other places. She looked him in the eyes. They had grown up in the same town. He'd known her as a girl until she left for Dana Hall and college. When he saw her after she returned already married, she wore the same warm expression when she shopped at Boynton's store, chaired library committee meetings, and read her own poems in public. He was married, and she was married, of course.

"It's Thanksgiving tomorrow," he said, and when she nodded, he looked at the floor. The deep blues and reds of the worn Persian carpet. When he stood, he focused on the dark oil portraits of her ancestors down the hall. He needed to be out of here, and he pushed himself from the table and limped (his knee aching again) down the hall past the door to the study. All those leather-bound volumes, her father's and her grandfather's books, which she'd read as a girl on summer afternoons when her mother propped open all the windows and the breeze from the river billowed the curtains and stirred the leaves of her father's newspaper resting on the arm of his chair. In the last year, she'd painted him a picture of her whole life.

She touched his back. "I'm sorry, John," she said, and for a moment he thought she would take back what she'd said. "I am sure you saw many horrible things." Her hand on his seemed to weigh more than any man could lift.

He nodded and limped as quickly as he could out the door. Not the first time he'd run for his life. On the granite landing, his heart jumped but didn't stop. He jog-hopped with his bad knee toward his tricycle. When he turned the trike around, he realized the battery was dead. He'd never be able to pedal—or walk, for that matter—up and over the hill to the house.

He hobbled around the edge of the woods. His breath seized every time a dry branch snapped under his boots. He had left the Dickinson in her kitchen, but he didn't think he would read any more Dickinson in the time he had left.

Isabel kept an old wooden rowboat down by the river for when her daughter and grandchildren visited. He spotted the upturned blue hull, made of plywood, half its paint gone. He flipped it over and found the gray oars rotting but still solid. Larry had pulled the dock for her already. With his back to the river, he tugged the boat a few feet at a time to the marshy shore. The tide would pinch anytime now. He waded up to his knees and pulled the boat in after him. Sensing Isabel watching him, he tried to climb quickly into the boat, but he couldn't raise his feet. He dove headfirst over the side and used his arms to right himself. When he craned his neck, he spotted her halfway between the river and her house and moving fast on her springy legs.

"John," he heard Sarah say in his ear, "why did you never tell me what you saw?"

"I just wanted to forget it," he said.

"John . . ." Isabel, calling his name. Though he'd launched himself into ebb tide, he did have the wind in his favor. Before he could set the locks and oars in place, he'd already drifted out of Isabel's view and traveled fifty yards, maybe seventy-five. Rowing, he picked up speed and felt the satisfying whoosh of the oars and the bow cleaving the water. He had rowed this stretch as a boy many times, and now all he wanted to do was get home to Sarah.

The three-story shops lined the waterfront. Behind their sagging roofs, the square captains' houses and church spires of town stretched up the hill toward the top of the valley, where his Puritan ancestors had arrived hundreds of years before to claim this shore—the farthest upriver into the belly of the state a deepwater vessel could travel. What had he done with the life they had prepared for him? Running around a field with a whistle, parsing lines of poetry for children who could think of nothing but chasing each other.

The men from the SS unit—five hundred, maybe—slipped into Austria, and from there he never knew what happened to them. Some might have been caught. Others must have escaped. John had been killing Germans since D-Day, and now his commanders told him to stop. Just like that.

The boat was leaking. Up to his ankles now. Nothing he could do but row harder. The rotten oar cracked, and his shoulder seized with pain. He sighted the field in front of his house and gave an extra-hard tug. A small person stood at the shoreline shielding his eyes. His great-grandson, Will, shouted, "Grand, grand," over the water. "What are you doing?"

John thought he would save his wind and attempt to answer the question later. The technique he'd used with his children and grandchildren, of putting them off until they forgot their questions, never worked with Will, who remembered everything and had a backlog of unanswered—and frequently unanswerable—questions that he brought to bear with a tax assessor's persistence. Will's mother, the doctor, had placed a stick in the ground to mark the spot past which her son should not venture closer to the water. Will leaned against the stick like a ballplayer leaning on his bat.

The boat nudged into the grass. The water had come to within six inches of the gunnel.

"There's a problem with your boat," Will observed from the safety of his position on the bank.

John stood in the shallows of the river and looked up at Will's blue eyes and unruly hairdo.

"I wish I could ride in the boat with you," Will said sadly. He pursed his lips. Despite his California origins, possibly Will had inherited a tendency to look at all boats, even this boat, with longing. "My mother thinks I'm going to the bathroom." Will turned his miniature hand palm up. "I was going to the bathroom, but then I looked out the window and saw *you* in the river. In that boat," Will said.

When John tried to trudge through the mud, his boots stuck and wouldn't move. He undid the laces and pulled. The socks stayed with the boots as he freed his feet and fought the reeds to solid ground. The bank remained, and his right knee and now his hip had stopped working altogether. His back, his neck, his ribs—his whole body ached and burned and resisted taking one more step. He stumbled, turned his ankle and scraped his forehead on a root.

14

"You didn't make it!" Will said, more thrilled than troubled, it seemed to John.

John grabbed the branches of a bush and pulled and crawled his way up the slope. At the top, he collapsed, wheezing, in front of Will, who looked from his face to his wet trousers and bare feet.

"You have blood on your head," Will said. He leaned close to John's face and frowned. In Will's genius private school, where they taught astrophysics to eight-year-olds, people didn't get knocked around. They didn't make emergency landings on hostile shores. John touched his forehead, and his fingers came away bloody.

"Here they come," Will said, pointing to the side of the house. The family had spotted him and started across the field. They would surround him.

"Stay here," Will said. "Take a time out. I will go tell them you're sleeping."

The black soles of Will's shoes snapped as he sprinted through the grass.

"Sarah?" John said and looked for her in the apple trees his father had planted along the shore, in the windows of the house at the head of the field, in the rowboat, submerged to the gunnels and turning in the current, and in the faces of his family waving to him from halfway across the field. They would want to know where he'd been. "Sarah," he said, no longer recognizing the sound of his own voice, "what do I tell them?"

He closed his eyes to listen for her answer and heard only silence.

The Last Voyage of the *Alice B Toklas*

(1981)

John Jacobs Howland, Sarah Libby Howland,
John Stoughton Howland

When, at fifteen, I began my career as the rural carrier associate of Howland Island, Maine, a post officer from the regional office showed up unannounced and reminded me that I must adhere to the agency's mission statement by ensuring the "prompt, reliable, and efficient" delivery of the mail. In August I thought of his words as I held the official-looking letter that had arrived for the writer staying in my grandparents' guest cottage. Most people only received bills and handwritten notes from friends and relatives. Sometimes a postcard. My grandfather, who frequently asked me if I'd heard the writer say anything interesting, would love to see the contents of a typed envelope from the Jonathon Riley Agency, 333a Lafayette St., New York, NY.

As I put the letter aside instead of in the writer's mailbox, I thought of the postal motto, which I had memorized the previous summer: *Neither snow, nor rain, nor heat, nor gloom of night stays these couriers from the swift completion of their appointed rounds.* Halfway through sorting the rest of the mail, I picked up the writer's envelope again and ran my finger over the indentations left by the typewriter on the letters of the writer's name, Alexander Smith, and the name of the island. The bell on the door clanged, and hard-soled shoes tapped down the hall to my office/candy store.

"Hey," the writer said. "Anything for me?" Through the dark glass of his Ray-Ban Aviators, he looked at me sitting on my swivel chair behind my desk complete with various cubbyholes for international, certified, and return service forms, as well as a number of rubber stamps I longed to use in an official capacity. I still held his envelope clamped between my thumb and forefinger.

"Is that mine?" he asked, his eyebrow rising above the gold rim of his glasses.

I nodded, relieved, and handed the envelope to him. He turned and walked away without saying goodbye.

The writer's vanilla-colored envelope would have leaned at an angle in his brass box. The weaker envelopes, especially the blue *par avion* ones, began to sag from moisture after a few hours. Made of thicker paper, the writer's letter hadn't even bent in the mailbag on the boat ride from the mainland.

At 1 p.m. I rushed home to eat the lunch Grandma had left for me. She'd taken the skiff to shop on the mainland, so I had a one-day reprieve from afternoon chores. The writer had only left fifteen minutes ahead of me, but when I arrived at our house and looked out the kitchen window across the field that stretched to the beach and the guest cottage, I saw no sign of him.

Most summers our house filled with cousins, uncles and aunts, and my sister, but for the last two weeks of August this year, I was alone with my grandparents. My sister was staying with my father and his new girlfriend over on China Lake, and my cousins were busy with their parents. I called out for my grandfather. When he didn't answer, I knew he was probably down at the island landing.

I had just finished the first half of my sandwich when the door to the guest cottage flew open and smacked against the shingles. The writer lurched into the field, kicked a rotting log with the toe of his leather shoe, and yelped as he hopped on one foot. In his balled fist, he raised a crumpled letter the same color as the envelope that had come for him and threw it toward the mouth of the bay.

The August winds on our part of the coast followed predictable patterns. The letter rose briefly, pushed a few inches, no more, toward the water, then slowly reversed course and blew back over his head. As he whipped the door to the cottage closed behind him, I watched the letter roll over the recently mowed field and pass by our house.

Over cod cakes that night, my grandfather smoothed the creases of the letter, took his reading glasses out of the pocket of his flannel shirt, and squinted at the contents. He read it once and raised his head to look out the row of windows at the bay. On the second read, he began to shake his head.

"What does it mean?" I said. I'd read it, of course. Something about his publisher not liking his second book. A former English teacher at the high school in Vaughn, where my whole family lived in the winter, my grandfather was our only authority on literary matters.

"It's not good news for him, that's for sure. This kind of thing happens all the time." My grandfather returned his glasses to his pocket, carefully folded the letter, and pushed it to the middle of the table. He sat back, cupped his hands behind his head. "Why don't you ask him to supper at the end of the week?" my grandfather said as he stood to retrieve more matches for his pipe. Among his few friends in Vaughn, my grandfather was known as "the Torso." A disproportionate amount of his long frame extended above the waist. Tall on foot, he towered when we all sat at the supper table, and when he walked, his head didn't bob, his shoulders didn't sway, and his perfectly erect posture held straight as a board.

"Should I mention the Aga stove?" I said. He didn't nod, because I'd come dangerously close to calling it what it was: John Updike's Aga stove. The stove on which John Updike had made tea in the morning before he sat down to write or grilled himself a cheese sandwich after a long day of writing. In our family, if you wanted to speak of John Updike, you spoke of "the stove," not, as Uncle Alden sometimes called it, "the Aga." Likewise, you could say "Lewiston" but nothing about the dowel factory my great-grandfather had bankrupted. Nothing about China Lake, where my father spent most of his time.

I saw the writer the next morning standing above the island landing. His hair stood up in back. Though drizzle pattered through the maples and fog sat right on the ground and showed no signs of blowing out, he wore his sunglasses. He hadn't shaved, and when he raised the lenses to squeeze the bridge of his nose, I saw bags under his eyes.

"You have any aspirin?" he said and leaned against the white oak that had long served as the anchor point for people to haul their boats at the end of the season. His slight paunch pushed against the front of his button-down shirt. The matching pouch of fat under his chin thickened when he yawned and squinted at me through his Ray-Bans. One of my goals in life at this point was someday to own a pair of real Ray-Bans. A friend at school told me I had to watch out because a lot of people would try to sell you fake ones.

"They . . ." he said, nodding at the one-room shack the association people called the yacht club. Despite the weather, "they" were setting up for the monthly yacht club lunch on the screened porch. "Are you one of them? You're not, are you?"

"No," I said quickly.

20

"You and . . . what's your name again?"

I'd told him three times already. "John."

"You and your grandfather and that other guy, the one with the beard . . . the carpenter."

He meant Uncle Alden.

"You're not like the rest of these people walking around in stupid-looking shorts."

Unlike those people, we were from here. We owned the original farmhouse on the island. We didn't live in it year-round, but our ancestors had.

"What you got there?" he asked, pointing at the paperback in my hand. I showed him the cover with the lighthouse.

"Ahh," he said, "that book." The writer scratched his chin. I could sense his eyes narrowing behind the lenses of his glasses. "John what?" he said eventually. "What's your last name?"

"Howland."

"Same as the island. They name the island after you?" He laughed, but this was not a subject of humor for us. The writer had stumbled upon my grandfather's greatest obsession, a grievance he had cultivated like a rose garden. We had lost most of the island in the 1800s when, one generation at a time, members of our family who needed money had sold off pieces to a summer colony now called the Howland Island Association. With his canvas bag in one hand and his pipe in the other, my grandfather often plowed right through gatherings of people in green shorts. He spurned their friendliness on the trail. He mutely refused invitations to parties.

"Are those Ray-Bans real?" I asked. He'd just asked me a lot of questions. I felt I was owed the truth about his sunglasses.

He took off his glasses and looked at the tiny cursive *Ray-Ban* scrawled on the lens. "I don't know. I hope so. I'll give them to you when I leave if you can keep these people around here away from me." He looked over his shoulder at the yacht club.

When she picked her mail up one day, Mrs. Hayes described the writer as having "ruined his looks through booze and neglect."

Someday I, too, wanted to be known as having "once been handsome." Mrs. Hayes, Sophie, who, roughly the same age as the writer, took exquisite care of herself and seemed to subsist on water and lettuce sandwiches and wore only tight, high-waisted floral shorts and pink IZOD shirts, closed her eyes before she spoke. She followed her statement by raising her chin and looking right at me.

When the writer pulled out an envelope, I thought for a moment he had somehow retrieved the letter I had picked up next to our house.

"I need you to mail this," he said and placed it carefully in my hands.

"But it doesn't have a stamp," I said.

"I know it doesn't have a stamp, champ. I didn't bring any with me on my preppy, mosquito-infested vacation. You're Postmaster Howland of Howland Island, right? Put a stamp on there for me, and I'll pay you back."

One of the Palfrey girls—Charlotte, the older one—stepped out of the yacht club and walked toward us with her arms crossed and chin tucked into her chest. Her long hair swung back and forth. I'd spent my life pretending to have no interest in her when she and her friends arrived from Massachusetts and New York for a month each August. According to my grandfather, the Palfreys were *carpetbaggers*—in 1939 they moved in next door and drove our taxes up. I'd once heard Grandma say under her breath that for all the people around us, paying taxes was like buying an ice-cream cone.

The writer watched Charlotte go for a minute and turned back to me.

"What're you waiting for?" he said. "Permission to speak?"

"My grandfather said you should come up to the house for supper," I said to change the subject. "We have John Updike's Aga stove."

The rain-splattered sunglasses had slipped down his nose. In the shallows behind the lenses, his eyelashes flicked like minnows.

22

"I don't understand," he said. "Your family knows John Updike?" I nodded, just slightly. "If I don't swim for the mainland first, I'll come for dinner. So what time do they pick up the mail here?"

I explained that it wasn't picked up—every day I had to take the mail to the mainland by skiff.

"So they let some kid in a leaky boat drag it across the high seas?" "I'm bonded," I said.

"No, you're not. You're a kid. Kids don't get bonded."

"How would you know?" I muttered.

"Listen . . ." he paused, looking either at the top of my head or over me. Could he have forgotten my name?

"John," I said.

"John, I didn't sleep too well last night."

I reminded him about supper Friday night. He seemed likely to forget.

"Yeah, I'll be there."

On Fridays my grandparents started drinking gin around noon and didn't stop until supper. The writer arrived at 5:30 carrying a bottle of wine and not wearing his sunglasses. Grandma's corgi, Emma, broke into a frenzy of barking. The writer held the bottle of wine out to Grandma, who snorted and snatched it out of his hand.

Uncle Alden, sitting on the far side of the porch in a dirty T-shirt and cutoffs, crossed his legs, pointed his bearded chin out toward the cove and the open ocean and bounced his black-soled foot in the air. When he first heard about the writer coming to supper, Uncle Alden, who claimed to have known plenty of writers at college (before he dropped out), said they were mostly full of shit. For money he worked on the island as a carpenter fixing people's cottages. His calling, as he put it, was to build chairs (shown at the Winnegance Gallery in Bath).

My grandfather shook the martinis and filled everyone's glasses while the writer settled into the wicker. With his cheeks freshly shaven, he seemed ten years younger. Every time he tried to lean back, he started to slip out of the chair. He looked, for a moment, like a student sitting in class.

"John here tells me you have John Updike's stove."

"We do, don't we?" my grandfather said and nodded at me.

My cue to talk about the merits of "the stove," its origins, its place in stove history: "The Aga stove was invented by Nobel Prize-winning physicist Gustaf Dalén, who lived from 1869 to 1937. Since 1930, they have been manufactured in England by the Aga Rangemaster Group. They were designed to make use of a low but continuously burning heat source."

My grandfather picked up with the general career of the inventor, Gustaf Dalén, who invented Agamassen, a substrate used to absorb hydrocarbon gas so it could be used safely in lighthouses—this, not the stove, had earned Dalén the Nobel Prize. The stove, a kind of afterthought, had made his career. Wasn't that often the case? My grandfather posed his question to the field in front of our house and to the bay and the ocean beyond. A rhetorical question meant solely for contemplation—I worried that the writer didn't understand the rules.

"I suppose you're right," the writer said. Uncle Alden stole a glance at the writer. "The view from your deck is amazing," the writer added. While he looked over the beach and across the bay to Hendricks Light, standing tall and luminous, we looked at him. The word "deck" hung in the air.

"It's in the kitchen," Uncle Alden said. "The stove."

My grandfather told the writer to come see for himself. I followed them into the kitchen. Cream-colored, with four heavy doors and a pipe that connected to the chimney, the stove took up one whole wall. Uncle Alden had constructed a separate support system under the corner of the kitchen. Grandma had rested a large silver platter on one of the burner covers, and sometimes in late summer a vase filled with sea heather perched on another cover.

"It's huge—the size of three stoves," the writer said, though its size would not have struck any of us as its most notable feature.

"Yuh," Grandma said with her eyes closed. Grandma hated the stove, which only worked for cooking if you kept it burning all the time, which you couldn't do in the summer (when we lived on the island) without turning the house into a Dutch oven. She would rather we used the stove as a mooring for the boat.

"It puts out a lot of BTUs if you bank the coal in the firebox," Uncle Alden said.

"Coal?" the writer said. "Do people use coal anymore?"

"One of the ovens is not working," my grandfather said. "I forget which one." He opened one door to reveal the firebox, another door to reveal one of the ovens. "Big enough for a turkey," he noted.

"I would never cook a turkey in this thing," Grandma said.

Finally, my grandfather opened the door he had wanted to open all along. He knew very well which one. "Oh, this is the one that doesn't work," he said and started to close the enameled hatch.

"Wait," the writer said, stepping forward and pointing. "Was that a pair of tennis shoes?"

My grandfather slowly reopened the door and peered in as if he'd forgotten about the shoes.

"Oh, yes, they were there when we got the stove. We leave them in there to remind us which oven not to use."

"Are those?" The writer laughed and raised his eyebrows to express exactly the kind of surprise my grandfather hoped for. Instead of answering, my grandfather opened the stove door wider. From the side, you could see that the instep of one shoe had worn at a bevel, and the sun-faded canvas tops had been scuffed near the laces. "Updike's shoes?" the writer said. He leaned over with his hand outstretched. For a moment I feared he might try to touch the shoes. No one, not even my grandfather, touched the shoes. The writer seemed to realize he was about to cross a line and retracted his hand.

I knew what would come next.

"So you went down and picked the stove up?" the writer said. "I mean, how? It must weigh as much as a subway car."

My grandfather smiled, and the writer pretended to look at the stove from the side, from above, from the front again, though he was really looking at the tennis shoes.

"So you know him—Updike?" the writer asked.

My grandfather straightened himself, crossed his arms over his chest, and gazed at the tennis shoes.

"Well, he and I were at Harvard, and several years ago we had a call about the stove, so we drove down to Prides Crossing."

"Is he much of a tennis player?" the writer asked.

"You certainly wouldn't think so to look at him," my grandfather said.

As we all passed through the dining room to the parlor, the writer gazed at the cracked plaster, paintings, handmade furniture, the long varnished sweep oar nailed to the ceiling beams along with at least 150 corks from a century of New Year's eve parties held around the hearth. I could see the stories about our lives forming in the writer's head.

"What happened to your drink?" my grandfather asked him.

"I don't know!" the writer said. He smiled as my grandfather poured him another from the silver shaker and refilled my grandmother's cup. The writer leaned over one of my grandmother's paintings of Five Islands.

"I like this a lot," he said with more enthusiasm than I'd seen him express about anything. His shoulders straightened as if a monkey had finally climbed off his back.

My grandfather settled on the sofa. "She calls it her attempt at something and then tells me it will end up in the attic. Or destroyed."

"I don't know about that!" Grandma protested.

"Do you have a gallery?" the writer asked as he looked around the room at her other paintings.

Instead of answering, Grandma stuck her hand out in front of her, extended her fingers, and clamped them around her cup. My grandparents drank martinis from metal cups. She had been the head of the school board in our area and didn't call herself an artist.

"She doesn't do that," my grandfather said curtly.

"Do what?" the writer asked. "Sell her work?"

Grandma squeezed her eyes shut and twitched her head to the right—a form of "no" too emphatic for words.

"No one wants this stuff," she said.

"She's just like her grandfather, who did those over there," my grandfather said and pointed to the far wall. "Lived to be 105. A worshipper of the obdurate truths, I believe he would have said of himself."

"Jesus, what're you talking about?" Grandma said.

"You sign them Sarah Libby," the writer said.

"That's who I was before him," Grandma said and nodded her head toward the far side of the sofa.

"She would've been something if she hadn't married me and spent all her time working and raising children."

"I would have gone on a car trip to New Brunswick with my cousin Janet. Instead, I married you."

"I'll take you to New Brunswick," my grandfather said. "We'll drive up in September."

She took a sip from her drink. At moments like this, with my grandparents distracted and no other cousins around, I had learned to dip into the kitchen for my own cocktail. Six parts gin to two parts orange juice. I sucked down half the glass, filled it back up, and headed for the parlor, where the writer walked along the bookshelves. Uncle Alden had disappeared, drifting like a dark cloud back to his home across the water, which was fine with me.

"These are all written by Douglas Libby," the writer said.

"Her uncle," my grandfather said, raising a finger and pointing across his chest at Grandma, "grew up over there and joined the French Foreign Legion in 1914."

"I know this guy," the writer said. "I mean I know of him."

"He was known, I think," my grandfather said.

"He was a drunk," Grandma said.

My grandfather tilted his head. "He wrote like someone who never read anything after Balzac."

Grandma held out her cup. My grandfather shook the empty pitcher, raised both elbows, and paused with his eyes fixed on the last light painting the bay. He groaned slightly, stood fully upright, and glided toward the kitchen.

When my grandfather returned from the kitchen, pitcher in hand, he paused above me. I didn't have to look up to see his scowl. I'd left the gin bottle next to the kitchen sink, not on the table, where it belonged.

"Leave him alone," Grandma said. "He's a good boy."

"Ahhhhhh! But he's not a good boy," my grandfather said as he poured Grandma a new drink. He splayed the fingers of his free hand and lowered my grandmother's drink to the coffee table with exaggerated care. When the cup finally came to rest on the table, he lifted both his hands, then sat down with a sigh. Emma shifted far enough away from him not to be crushed.

The writer pointed at a painting Grandma had done of me sitting on the porch with a book on my lap looking out to sea. The very opposite of the 150-year-old paintings on the second floor of my young, square-jawed ship-captain ancestors sitting upright with compasses or charts in their laps.

"Is that you, postmaster?" the writer said.

I nodded.

"What book are you reading there?"

"A prop, I think," my grandfather said.

Grandma vanished into the kitchen and a short time later announced supper, which worried me. The quality of Grandma's fish cakes suffered after five hours of drinking, but semi-inebriation was the only state in which she would agree to feed people outside the family.

When the writer offered to help her carry in the food, Grandma pretended not to hear. My grandfather sat at the head of the table, crossed his legs at the knees, folded his hands in his lap, and angled his chin to the south, straight out to sea. Many of us in the family had been born with round faces and button noses; not my grandfather. Even in his seventies, his head stood high and square on his shoulders like a bust on a mantel. One of Grandma's paintings captured this moment, right before supper.

I hoped he would tell the story of how one of our many ship-captain ancestors from Vaughn had spent a year as a prisoner of Barbary pirates in the 1700s. The feel of the wool shirt and the weight of the iron shackled to his ankle. Anyone caught trying to escape was thrown from the walls of the city by the dey's men, or they might be tied in a sack with rocks and thrown into the Mediterranean.

Having arranged his napkin properly on his lap, my grandfather then never used it. He cut his food with surgical precision and never lowered his head toward his plate. I tried to imitate him. Emma circled his chair with her nose to the ground. Grandma, whose drinking angled toward the sentimental conviction that she'd been blessed with an extraordinarily talented and adoring family, looked as if she wanted to hug someone. I wanted to hug her, too.

The writer asked my grandfather what he was currently reading.

"*Don Quixote*," my grandfather said.

"Oh, really? Which translation?" the writer asked.

My grandfather had read the novel in Spanish and in every English translation. He didn't answer right away as he passed the fish cakes to the writer and took a piece of bread for himself.

"I reread it a few years ago," the writer said, and my grandfather's eyebrow twitched.

"Don Quixote hears all things speaking. Sancho Panza is the practical materialist," my grandfather said.

The writer paused with the fork in his hand. "Yes," he said.

"Unfortunately, the death of Don Quixote marks the rise of Sancho."

"How so?" the writer asked.

My grandfather smiled. "The rise of prose," he said. "Stuff. More and more stuff. Have you ever been out on the water?" he said.

"Out there?" the writer asked, pointing toward the open ocean, now covered in darkness.

"Tomorrow, we'll take him by the lighthouse," my grandfather said and nodded to me.

"I have to admit I'm afraid of the water," the writer said as he stared out the window.

"Nonsense," Grandma said and scooped another barely cooked fish cake onto his plate.

On the dock the next day, Grandma looked over the writer from head to foot as if she had just noticed him for the first time.

"I met your neighbors up the hill," the writer said.

"The Palfreys? They're from New Hampshire. They haven't been coming here long."

"Really? I thought the woman said . . ."

Grandma waved her hand in the air. "Helen, I don't care what she told you. She's French, you know. Michaud. Says her people were connected to Pierre L'Enfant." Grandma looked at the writer with her eyebrows raised.

"The guy who built Washington, DC?"

"You believe that?"

The writer shrugged, and Grandma turned away.

I lowered myself into the stern of the small punt while my grandfather held the oars in place with his elbows and knees and lit his pipe. Smoke rose in a cloud that hung around my head as he rowed us. Under the black metal letters ALICE B TOKLAS screwed onto the planks of the stern of our boat, you could still see the outline of the name BETSY, the wife of the man, Harold Moore (a distant cousin to my grandfather), who built her and ran her as a lobster boat for almost thirty years. The iron fastenings wept dark rust stains down the sides of the peeling white hull.

Right before we reached the stern, my grandfather let go of the oars, stood up on the seat of the punt, and leaped onto the deck. Without a glance in my direction, he buried his head in the engine compartment. My grandfather had the air of someone who could fix anything, but the last time we'd refueled, Bobby Plumber at Five Islands Marine had told my grandfather not to take "the old girl farther from shore than you can swim." She had twice slipped her mooring in the last ten years because of rot around the cleat. The main problem with the *Alice B*, which for some reason never seemed to worry my grandfather, was that she was sinking. The electric pump ran day and night.

The *Alice B* had no neutral, just forward and reverse. Grandma knew the drill. As we approached the dock, she positioned the writer in front of her. When my grandfather swung us around parallel with the dock only a foot away, Grandma shooed the writer into the boat. He landed on his knees, and we swung around for our second pass to get Grandma, who simply lifted her foot and stepped forward as if onto a moving escalator.

As we rounded the north point, my grandfather pointed into the woods above the beach. "That's where my ancestors built their first house." At low rpms, the engine that lived under the wooden box amidships jackhammered while the exhaust pipe sticking up through the roof buzzed like a giant insect.

We headed for open water, and my grandfather opened up the throttle to 4500 rpms, the sweet spot where the engine reached a gallop. As he searched for his tobacco in one pocket and his pipe in the other, I reached for the wheel to keep us on course. The *Alice B* pulled to starboard, especially at speed. He nestled against the windshield to light his pipe and without glancing at me took the wheel again. I let go just as a cloud of pipe smoke mushroomed around his head. We passed Joey Pinkham hauling with his son off Bull Ledge. In the middle of sorting through one of his pots, Joey raised an arm, then tossed out several shorts. In reply, my grandfather raised his hand in the air.

Hendricks Light came into view. Rollers split aqua green over the axe head of the granite point.

"There it looms," my grandfather said, "stark and straight, white bricks glaring." As I followed the writer's eyes, I wondered how he must see the lighthouse on his first day ever on the water, his first time up close.

The swells lengthened and the *Alice B* settled into a steady roll with spray feathering across the windshield and the deck. My grandfather told the story of riding out Hurricane Carol in the Bay of Fundy in 1952, a story I'd heard from Grandma before. In Baddeck, on the island of Cape Breton, Nova Scotia, where he and his friends picked up a schooner, they stayed at an inn where all the maids were blue-eyed Irish girls. When my grandfather gestured to where the waves crested fifty feet above the deck, the writer looked up and said he couldn't believe anyone would survive that. For a moment I was there with him on that schooner in 1952, my bloody hands hauling on the jib sheet while he lashed the tiller so we could heave to into the path of the storm.

As we rounded the western tip of Damariscove Island, Grandma, sitting on a metal lawn chair in the stern with her eyes closed and her chin raised to the sky, pulled her sweater tight over her shoulders. In less than a month, the summer would be over and we would all be back in Vaughn, sliding toward winter. My sister and I living with my grandparents half the time and my mother the rest of the time, my father living over on China Lake with his new girlfriend. In the winter, trudging up the hill to school and working on the woodpile in the afternoons, I felt as if the story of our lives came to a halt until we returned to the island.

To enter the only harbor of Damariscove Island you had to avoid the wide, sharp ledges on both sides of the approach. The narrow harbor extended far into the island, which had been tree-less for as long as I could remember. Because of the high hills on both sides, the water in the harbor remained calm while the surf pounded the windward shore.

We landed at the dock and climbed the ramp. I waited for my grandfather to tell the writer, as he had told others, that the first Howland in America set foot here in 1621, when he came to beg help for the starving pilgrims at Plymouth. Without this tiny island, and without John Howland, they all would've died.

My grandfather carried the basket up the trail that wound past the Coast Guard station. Grandma spread the plaid blanket on the high grassy point where we always ate and anchored the corners with stones. The basket contained sandwiches, the martini shaker, and molasses cookies wrapped in a cloth. My grandfather poured into the small tin cups. Instead of sipping his right away, he rested his cup on his knee. We all sat facing the bay. At a distance of several miles, the pointed firs sat above the line of pale granite.

"The shinbone coast," my grandfather said.

I bit into my cheese sandwich, which Grandma had lined with yellow mustard, and I began to imagine the story the writer would tell about us. No heroes, battles, murders, discoveries, ship-wrecks—all of that would be in the background.

My grandfather took the pipe out of his mouth and pointed at the *Alice B.*

From a distance, you couldn't see the paint peeling or the hull losing its shape on the starboard side. Planks could be replaced, but when the ribs warped, no one would be able to save her.

"Stein left most of her money to Toklas," he said, "and the paintings in the apartment in Paris, but their relationship had no legal status. When Toklas was away, Stein's family came in and stole them all. Toklas wrote her own memoir, you know. Even though she wrote it almost twenty years after Stein's death, the memoir stops the day Stein died, 1946."

"I didn't know that," the writer said.

"She had to live a lot of years as no one."

With the stem of his pipe still pointing at the harbor, the corners of his mouth turned down, my grandfather nodded.

"She was Stein's Sancho Panza," he said.

The writer stared at the sandwich my grandmother had made from stale bread and cheese she stored in the cupboard. Guests were always my grandfather's idea, never Grandma's. She served them food not even a squirrel would touch. The writer stuck out his tongue, touched the edge of the sandwich, and frowned. His hunger had yet to overcome his standards.

"So what happened when you drove down to Prides Crossing?" the writer asked.

My grandfather lifted his cup to his lips, sipped, set it down again. I sat up straight because my grandfather rarely told the story of picking up the stove. I'd only heard it once before from his mouth and only secondhand otherwise.

As my grandfather described John Updike, reading glasses dangling from his neck, answering the door, the writer raised his cup to his lips, and in my memory of the story (at least the version told on this day), John Updike said, "John! It's been years."

My grandfather finished his drink, got up, stretched his arms in the air, nodded to the writer, and said, "Come on," which I knew meant without me. I told myself I didn't need to go. Even though I knew exactly what my grandfather would say as he and the writer stood on the ledge above the Coast Guard station, I shuffled in their direction until I could hear just enough to follow what I'd already heard before. John Updike stands in the doorway of his Prides Crossing house. My grandfather asks if it's a bad time, but John waves my grandfather's worries away and comments that he has been praying for an excuse to abandon *Rabbit Redux*. The new Mrs. Updike greets my grandfather and Uncle Alden, and they sit on the patio and have drinks. My grandfather and John talk about their former classmates from Harvard and what has happened to them. After an hour or so, my grandfather says they have a long drive back to Maine and should see about the stove before they drink too much to do anything about it. John says he can't wait to get rid of the goddamned thing, which is too complicated, too big, too English. He suggests they hook up a chain to my uncle's truck and drag it out of the house. For a moment some version of this plan is seriously considered—with a blanket and maybe an old pair of skis underneath, such a thing might be possible. John Updike, a bit "shellacked," goes up to the attic for his old skis. In the end everyone gives up and decides to head into town. Over a third bottle of wine at supper, John insists that my grandfather and uncle stay the night.

As the writer and my grandfather walked back to the blanket, the wind whipped the words out of my grandfather's mouth and carried them out to sea. Interested in whatever my grandfather had said, the writer stopped walking and watched my grandfather—the first time I'd seen him really pay attention to anyone on the island.

"What did you say to him?" the writer asked.

"What could I say? He was right. I knew he was right. He knew he was right."

"So you said nothing."

"No! I told him to give someone else a chance."

The writer rocked back on his heels.

"I guess he didn't listen to you."

"No, he did not."

The writer and my grandfather settled on the ground next to Grandma and me, topped off their drinks, and picked up their sandwiches. My grandfather ate his, while the writer sniffed around the edges again.

Knowing that my grandfather had never even met John Updike didn't matter to me. I believed the story of picking up the stove, though I knew it wasn't true. Uncle Alden had once pointed out that the old man and Updike were not even at Harvard together—once he showed me the Red Book to prove it. Uncle Alden had gone to college briefly with a friend of John Updike's son, which was how he had heard about the stove. He and my grandfather hadn't even gone to Prides Crossing—they'd picked the stove up at a garage in Ipswich.

The day my grandfather and Uncle Alden drove into Five Islands with the stove, the fishermen gathered around the wharf as my grandfather brushed pine needles off the top and reached into one pocket for his tobacco pouch and another for his pipe and matches. The wind had come up early that day, out of the north at fifteen knots, so it took three matches to get the pipe lit. Then he put his arm over my shoulder.

When Harold Pinkham asked how much the stove had cost, my grandfather uttered the single most impressive word in our language: "Free." Not just any stove, my grandfather explained, an Aga stove, the most indestructible stove ever made. We backed the truck up to the edge of the wharf. While people stood watching, the loading winch used to haul crates of lobster to the deck lowered the stove into the stern of the *Alice B.* We motored north along the shore toward the island with several lobster boats in tow. It would take six men to muscle the stove onto the dock, six more from the island to lift it into the back of the island truck. Grandma had set out bottles of Poland Spring gin on the porch.

My grandfather inhaled and said, "I've been working on a little book myself."

Grandma almost choked, and I lowered my sandwich into my lap. We'd never heard such a thing.

"What about?" the writer said casually.

"It's nothing, really, a few questions about *Quixote* that have bothered me over the years," he said. "You see, Cervantes created a character greater than the book from which the Don wandered. How is it that the knight commits the same chivalric errors in taste that Cervantes is so eager to criticize? In Don Quixote's speeches about becoming a knight-errant, there is no irony. The only difference between Don Quixote and Lancelot and Sir Tristram is that Don Quixote lived in the age of gunpowder, and he could find no knight to fight. It's not a satire at all. It's a condemnation of a world in which the virtues of the knight cannot be recognized."

The writer nodded while my grandfather picked at the grass between his knees, pretending to seem relaxed, I could tell, as he waited for the writer to finish sipping from his cup.

"You may have something there," the writer said. "But what do I know?"

"As much as anyone, I'm sure. The fun sinks to the low level of medieval farce: donkeys, gluttons, tormented animals, bloody noses. Cervantes put up with the Inquisition, solemnly approved of his country's brutal attitude toward Moors. The art of a book is not necessarily affected by its ethics, wouldn't you say?"

"Yes, I guess that's true," the writer said.

After a few moments of silence, my grandfather rose to his feet again and walked toward the water to light his pipe. The writer finished the rest of his drink and followed him. With the stem of his pipe, my grandfather pointed to Newagen Harbor, Fisherman's Island to the east, Seguin Island to the west. Before I could catch up to them, I heard the words "gilded butterflies."

Grandma called for me to come back and sit down. I obeyed, as I almost always did with her, and I heard nothing more because the wind increased as it did every afternoon in August. My grandfather spoke with more intensity, and the writer leaned in.

"Eat the rest of your lunch," Grandma said behind me, "or you're not having any of these cookies."

I was sure the writer would forget, but as we passed the channel nun in the *Alice B* on his last day, he tapped my shoulder with the folded Ray-Bans.

"You earned them," he said.

I hadn't, but that didn't matter to me. I had to exercise all my willpower not to put them on right away. I had a clear image of what I would look like wearing them. A younger version of the writer, a man on the verge of ruining himself.

When we reached Five Islands, my grandfather killed the engine so we could coast in to the dock. The writer hauled his suitcase over the gunnel and climbed out of the boat with the care of someone pulling himself back over the lip of a cliff. "Okay," he said when he was on his feet again. He reached over the boat and took my grandfather's hand in both of his.

"Send me the manuscript when you finish. I mean it," he said to my grandfather, who removed his pipe and nodded.

I managed to wait until we rounded the point before slipping the Ray-Bans over my nose. Behind the darkened glass, I watched boats pull at their moorings' tethers and seagulls glide over the evergreens running north to south on the island—the world I knew enhanced through a pulsating yellow tint.

After the writer left, my grandfather spent every morning, even Saturdays, in his bedroom with the door closed. The first half hour of quiet ended with a flurry of key taps and the sound of his chair scraping deeper grooves into the pine floor. Another lull always ended with a second burst of tapping that usually steadied for an hour, sometimes more, and fell off. Over supper he talked about the knight's library burning down. The loss of all those words.

Grandma and I met Mrs. Palfrey on the way to the landing, and she asked, in a whisper, how my grandfather's Don Quixote book was going. I had no idea how she'd found out. Maybe the writer had told someone, probably Sophie Hayes. I hadn't told anyone. No one would ever ask my grandfather about the book. "I can hear him typing from my porch," Mrs. Palfrey said. My grandfather typed with the window open, and the sound carried through the woods early in the morning before the wind rose. "You should mind your own business," Grandma snapped.

One after another, people from the island came to see me at the post office and asked me about the Quixote book. I became the expert for the remaining weeks of the summer. What was it about? How was the work going? I told them the book seemed to be going very well but that he wouldn't talk about it to anyone. "That's usually how it is with those things," I said. "If you talk about it to anyone, it goes away."

"I'm not surprised that he's writing a book, your grandfather," Mrs. Hayes said. "He's always seemed like a writer to me."

Uncle Alden did not let me off easily.

"What do you know about this book?" he asked me. He and his friends were rebuilding a porch on the other side of the island, and he had walked to the post office on his lunch break. I shrugged and pretended to busy myself rearranging the *par avion* envelopes.

"When did he tell you about it?" He stood over me with his arms crossed over his chest.

"Two weeks ago, I guess," I said, even though my grandfather and I had never talked about the book.

"He just told you out of the blue? For no reason?"

I shrugged again.

"How long has he been working on it? Don't shrug this time."

"A while, I would say."

"A while, you would say! You're starting to sound like him." He looked at his watch and rushed out.

Though my grandparents handled all their mail at their winter house in Vaughn, where they returned once every week or two, I thought my grandfather might mail chapters of the book to the writer from the island. He visited me at the post office once and left money for a Hershey bar, but he said nothing about his book or sending a letter. When he left, I went to the window. He stepped carefully on the old stairs and, partway down the trail, steadied himself against a tree for a moment before continuing.

When my grandfather finished his book, it would travel over the water to the writer and then to a publisher. His name would stretch across the spine, and the book would sit on shelves in libraries and in people's houses all over the state. People would take the book down and read the words he had typed in our house on the island. Though I knew we had no connection to John Updike, I pictured him reading my grandfather's book by the fire in Prides Crossing.

As far as I knew, he'd never tried to compose anything more than a letter before the writer came to visit, but when people on the island asked me about his book, I could tell that they believed it existed. It seemed obvious to them. Mrs. Palfrey, Mrs. Hayes— their belief cost them nothing, but I knew that in another two weeks I'd be sitting in my grandparents' peeling house in town with its sagging window mullions and the humming refrigerator containing discount cuts of meat.

At the end of the month, my grandparents rose early and prepared to take the *Alice B* upriver to Vaughn for the weekend. I rushed their bags down to the dock ahead of them. With one eye on the trail, I quickly searched the bags but saw no sign of the manuscript. When they appeared around the corner, walking slowly (more slowly every year now) with the dog between them, their arms were empty.

For lunch that day I cooked the last hot dog on the iron skillet and ate it with Grandma's potato salad at the kitchen table. With my stomach so full that I felt slightly dizzy, I stood in front of my grandparents' bedroom door, left partially ajar, and pushed the door open all the way with my foot. My grandfather's desk sat on the far side of the room under the eaves. Lowering myself into his chair, I looked out the window and rested my fingers on the enamel keys of the typewriter. Either the letters danced on the page, my grandfather had said, or they lay down. You either had the trick, or you did not.

Inside the slant-front desk I found stacks of paper crammed into drawers and slots. I pulled them out one at a time and looked for any sign of the typing I'd heard every morning. A few of the dusty, yellowing pages contained yearly tax amounts, lumber bills, food bills by the month. The top drawer held stacks of typed letters. From the pile, I found a letter dated three days ago and addressed to the Tax assessor of the town of Georgetown, Maine, Ronald Boynton, concerning property tax values on the island. In one section my grandfather outlined what he received for his taxes purely in the negative: *I do not receive road maintenance, I do not receive access to schools, I do not receive fire and medical services. What I do receive is a tax bill. My contribution to the creation of this single page of purple prose (and the in-depth analysis behind the eloquence) is exactly $600 dollars this year, $570 the year before, $530 the year before that. Cognizant though I am of the scarcity of trees for making paper in the State of Maine, a scarcity so severe that it would precipitate a 7.02% and 5% year-over-year inflation rate, and bearing in mind also that the ink used to print said bill is not produced in the State of Maine and has to be imported by tractor trailer overland from Worcester (and understanding as I do that the price of stamps increased last year by one cent), I fail to see why I should pay you any goddamned money at all. Instead of entertaining your incessant and unsubstantiated demands for more and more and more money without end into the future, I propose that you submit a request to me for funds that includes a detailed justification (beginning with why the tax assessor's position should exist) and ending with the word "please": early 14th c., "to be agreeable." From Old French plaisir, which means "to give pleasure, to satisfy." 11c., from Modern French plaire, from Latin placer, "to be acceptable, be liked, be approved," possibly from plak-e-, "to be calm," still water, etc., from root plak-, "to be flat." See "placenta": a circular organ in the uterus of pregnant eutherian mammals, nourishing and maintaining the fetus through the umbilical cord. Not to be used as the intransitive "do as you please" first recorded in Scotland (of all places) 1500; nor as the imperative "please do this" first recorded in England 1620 (of all times). Only, in this case, to beg, to wit: "PLEASE send SOME of the money without which I would have to look for another island with a shortage of overpaid, unskilled civil servants."*

The letter to the tax assessor was clearly a draft with crossed-out and penned-in sections. He had typed, edited, and probably retyped it.

In the bottom drawer, I found a cloth-covered yellow volume, *Lectures on Don Quixote,* by Vladimir Nabokov. The corners had worn down to the boards, and the pages hung loosely in their binding. I flipped through some of the dog-eared pages and found this: *Come with me ungentle reader who enjoys seeing a live dog inflated and kicked around like a soccer football, who likes on his way back from church to poke his stick at a poor rogue in the stocks, come with me and consider into what ingenious and cruel hands I shall place my ridiculously vulnerable hero.*

I read from other places marked in the book and came to a familiar passage underlined in pen: *Don Quixote is not a satire of the chivalric and romantic, it is a condemnation of a world in which the virtues of the knight cannot be recognized.*

I remembered exactly where I had sat next to Grandma (the feel of the cheese sandwich in my hand, the sharp granite under my butt, the smell of the salt air, the view of the bay) when my grandfather had spoken these words to the writer. As if I had been reading someone's personal diary, I carefully placed the book in the drawer exactly as I had found it. The air from the open window felt cool on the skin of my arm.

When we returned to Vaughn, where no one from town would be able to hear typing from the street and no one would ask about the progress of my grandfather's book, the mornings would be quiet again.

I looked out the window toward the small beach below the field. The two Palfrey sisters were rising out of the water. In the bright sun, the sea behind them was iridescent and dark, and their bathing suits shone as slick and black as sealskins.

As I walked downstairs and through the parlor, the sound of my bare feet slapping the pine boards echoed into every corner of the empty house. In the kitchen, I opened the oven door of the Aga stove, removed John Updike's tennis shoes, and slid my feet into place, one at a time. Pulling the laces tight, I wiggled my toes. I'd never played tennis, but it happened that I wore a size nine shoe.

With the Ray-Bans riding on the bridge of my nose, I crossed the field toward the beach, where the Palfrey sisters lay on their stomachs, their heads down and the soles of their feet angled to the sky. Standing next to a piece of driftwood, I gazed out and tried to think of what I could say to them about the sea rolling in waves of pure lemon to curve and swell upon the beach. I might say that at night the peaks climbing as high as church towers slowly ate away the ground where we stood.

The older one, Charlotte, rose on her elbow. Furrowing her brow, she glanced from the Ray-Bans to the tennis shoes.

"John," she said, "is that you?"

"No," I said in a voice I didn't recognize, a voice I'd been waiting to hear. "It's not."

Return of the Native

(1982)

John Jacobs Howland, Sarah Libby Howland,
Richard Dudley Saltonstall

Grandma appeared on the porch with her paints and her corgi, Emma. I sat upright with my prop, a book I wasn't reading, while Grandma made changes to her painting of me she had started the previous summer. Inside the front cover of the book, my great-grandmother had written her name, *Mary Hutchinson Fog*. "With a single drop of ink for a mirror, the Egyptian sorcerer undertakes to reveal to any chance comer far-reaching visions of the past," read the first line. Grandma reached out, dabbed at the curve of my jawline, and retracted the brush from the canvas, the last in a series featuring me gazing out to sea.

Out on the bay, Dickey Saltonstall bounced erratically toward us in his skiff. Dickey, who only took his misfiring outboard to the mainland when he had to, was an old friend of my family—their only friend among the summer people. For the last few years since my parents had split, he had also been my mother's boyfriend. Despite these marks against him, he was the only person on the island outside our immediate family whom I spent time with. A couple afternoons a week after my job running the island post office, I taught him how to sail.

Dickey's boat slapped a larger wave, and without warning he veered to the left and ground the bottom of his boat—and probably the prop—against the Turnip Island ledge. We could no longer hear the sound of his engine.

As the many times great-grandson of Captain Dudley Saltonstall, the colonial commander responsible for the disaster of the 1779 Penobscot Expedition, the worst American naval defeat of the American Revolution—the worst American naval defeat period until Pearl Harbor—Dickey'd had a lot of problems with boats over the years. Refusing to engage the British, Captain Saltonstall had led his fleet up the Penobscot River until they were trapped and battered to pieces. I considered myself a minor expert on American military defeats. Arrowsic and Kittery, if you counted colonists chased off the coast by the Abenaki, and Bunker Hill, Arnold's assault on Quebec. The Penobscot Expedition, so catastrophic in scale and so clearly the fault of one man (Dickey's namesake), remained my favorite.

Dickey set his oars and rowed toward the beach in front of our house. As he pulled his boat onto the sand and trudged through a tangled pile of seaweed the ocean had barfed up during the last storm, I thought of pictures I'd seen of Omaha Beach—not technically an American defeat, though it certainly was for those who'd landed there. My grandfather had survived the landing but never spoke of it.

"Dickey's been out of sorts since the letter from your mother arrived last week," Grandma said as she peered around her painting at the bay. Eight days ago, Dickey had received a letter with no return address. Just a stamp saying *Correos, Mexico Oficina Del Gobierno.* Wanting to hear how my mother had been doing in Batopilas (where she had been teaching English since the spring), and also needing to know when to pick her up at the airport, Dickey, Grandma, and I had been waiting for such a letter for weeks. According to the letter, she would arrive in Portland today on the last flight to land before midnight.

After lunch, Grandma asked me to find Dickey and remind him that we had to leave around 8 p.m. to pick my mother up at the airport on time. Because no one on the island had phones, I had to walk half a mile just to speak to him. Along the trail, I watched the summer light flip through the maple leaves. The two-hundred-acre island where my ancestors had settled in the late 1600s sat less than a quarter mile from the mainland, itself a larger island one could access by bridge, but I felt as if we lived far out to sea. No cars traveled the dirt paths of the island, just the truck run by the island caretaker. Except for the distant rumble of lobster boats in the bay, there was no sound. Salt mixed with pinesap pinched my nose. I wished my cousins were here. While I had stayed on the island to help Grandma, my grandfather had taken my younger sister and cousins upriver in our lobster boat to the town where we all lived in the winter. Along the way, they planned to stop at my favorite camping spot, on Swan's Island, where Benedict Arnold met with Abenaki Chief Swashan before pushing north to his doomed assault on Quebec.

I wanted to forget about my mother. I didn't miss her, exactly—she never seemed happy to see my sister or me. The three of us lived together like roommates in the old house in Vaughn. Less than three months ago Dickey, Grandma, my sister, and I had driven her to the airport in Portland, where, in the parking lot, my mother had squeezed my hand. "I'll see you again before you know it," she said to my sister and me and flicked her brown hair out of her face. Only thirty-nine, and thin as a girl, she had no gray hair. She didn't want us coming with her to the terminal—too emotional for her, she said, even though she was only going for the summer. We stood around the car and watched her pass, waving, through the revolving door.

Now the summer was almost over. In a few weeks everyone on the island except for the caretaker and my family would drive south to New York and Boston. All season the summer people had drifted from drinks on their porches to the landing to the apple orchard. On Sunday mornings at 10 a.m., when the chapel bell rang, they left their shingled cottages, funneled along the trail that passed by the post office, and filed into the pews to hear the summer minister speak of grace and service. My mother's father had been one of the visiting ministers back in the sixties; that's how my parents met.

I reached Dickey's house and peered through his screen door to where he sat in the dark parlor in a frayed chair. He told me to come in before I knocked and motioned to the other chair. I delivered the message Grandma had given me, and Dickey nodded. Lying beneath one of the front windows, Dickey's dog, Persephone, opened one eye but didn't raise her head. Dickey pushed out of his chair and ran his finger along the spines to select a record from his collection, which covered one whole wall in a homemade wooden shelf, painted purple. Next to the records was a bookcase filled with old books, including *Adam Bede*, the book I used as my prop for Grandma's painting, sitting next to *Scenes of Clerical Life* and *Return of the Native*.

He carried one of the records like a baby over to his turntable. Unlike us, Dickey had electricity, a hot water heater, blown-in insulation. Though he rarely spent it, especially on clothing, Dickey had money. Long before I came along, our family had forgiven him this fact. If he wasn't quite one of us, at least he wasn't one of them—the people who came to the island from out of state. He had been born in Portland.

"Do you remember the Gulf of Tonkin?" he asked.

"No," I said. He was referring to a naval battle, I knew that much. I was embarrassed to admit that was all I knew. He furrowed his brow as he did when he talked, during our sailing lessons, about the historical forces that would someday recalibrate social inequity.

"The trouble with your mother all started with Tonkin. I don't think you were born yet when she said those things to your grandfather about the war—it wasn't even a war then."

When my parents were still together, my mother and grandfather stayed on opposite sides of the room from each other during family events.

"Your grandfather was a soldier," Dickey said, "and on some level all soldiers think alike. And your mother was a moth in the firelight, you know what I mean?"

I nodded, though I had no idea.

"Then there was the night your grandfather threw the ham through the window. You were only about three years old then, right before your mother went out to San Francisco for six months."

I'd never heard of my grandfather doing such a thing, and I'd never heard of my mother going to San Francisco at all. I asked why she'd gone, though what I really wanted to know was why I didn't know she had disappeared for such a long time when I was so young.

"She rolled west *amid the wilds, the rocks, the storm and wintry night. . . .* We didn't know where she went at first, but I wasn't surprised that she'd gone. Sometimes people just disappear, John. Your father and mother were part of this crowd. A lot of them disappeared. Andrew Young, one of the people your father lives with over on China Lake. And your mother's friend Stacey Robinson, also a friend of mine. She still lives out in San Francisco, I think, but not in an apartment, not in a house. I was part of that crowd, too, though I was too old to be. I've always been too old to be doing whatever it is I'm doing." Dickey rubbed his eyes. Maybe he'd forgotten I was there.

"What did my mother say in her letter?" I asked. I found myself whispering, even though there was no one around. Dickey had told us when my mother's flight was supposed to arrive, but he hadn't shown us the letter. He had said the letter was short—information about her travel. I just needed to know that she was coming back, a need I wished I could live without.

Dickey shook his head with his eyes closed. "When your mother went out to San Francisco, your father wouldn't go after her, and neither would your other grandfather, the minister. They gave up on her. So I went. And, I have to tell you, people *loved* her out there. She still had that accent from Castine. I wish you could've seen her. She was the queen out there. She wanted everyone—all people—to be free. It wasn't just talk with her." Dickey bobbed his head. "She *felt* it. And in the middle of this batshit circus, she raised people out of their chrysalis. Not everyone, though," he said, nodding gravely, "not herself. She got arrested at People's Park. I was there. They were jealous of her flame."

The mother I knew took hour-long baths, blasted Neil Young until 1 a.m. on school nights, and heated up supper from cans. In the morning she guzzled coffee and never cooked breakfast.

"Your mum knew I was there to bring her back. *You can't rescue me,* she told me. For as long as I've known her—when she first came here with her parents those two summers her father was the island minister—she's dreamed of escaping. You have to understand the way she grew up in Castine, a smaller town than Vaughn, an only child living in that tiny house next to the vestry. Anyway, she did come back, but not because of me. She was starting to show with your sister by then."

"What did my mother's letter say?" I repeated.

Dickey steepled his hands in front of his mouth. "It was a very hard decision for her, going down to Mexico. She asked me to keep an eye on you. . . . The men wear skirts down there and drink beer made from these tiny seeds." Dickey pinched his thumb and forefinger together. "I've been there, when I was young. You really can't believe the place exists until you see it. And you can't really get there—it's at the bottom of this canyon deeper than most mountains are tall. Palm trees grow out of the foundations of ruined buildings."

I had pictured my mother living in an apartment, like the one where Dickey lived in Bath, and taking the bus to a schoolhouse. Dusty streets, maybe palm trees.

"She said she was going to be teaching."

"I'm sure she is," Dickey said, raising his eyebrows.

The record ended and the arm of the player slid to its cradle, but the humming continued in Dickey's throat. He leaned back in his chair and gazed out the window at the field that ran from in front of his house to the western shore of the island. The grass warbled across the two-hundred-year-old warped windowpanes that always looked wet, especially in the sunlight.

Dickey described the rest of what my mother had said in the letter he'd received from her: she washed her clothes in the river with herders. The canyon walls eclipsed the sun early in the afternoon. She'd met a woman, an artist from Germany who lived in a one-room adobe studio and walked through the canyons on sandals she had made from old tires.

Dickey stood, lifted the needle off the record, and slowly shuffled to the kitchen, where I heard him put on the kettle and open the breadbox.

By the time I reached the edge of his field, the music returned—the same record. When I stepped onto the porch of our house, I smelled hamburger—early supper and a treat any day of the week, any time of the year, even though the meat had to have been excavated from under the melting block of ice in the wooden icebox.

"What did he say?" Grandma asked from the kitchen.

"Not much," I said.

Grandma grunted and set a plate of cod cakes at her place and a burger on a chipped blue plate in front of me. I leaned over to check for signs of rot, but she'd burned both sides black. I asked if we had any buns, and she found half a hot-dog bun, which she dropped on top of the meat. Now that I'd asked for it, I had to eat it. Before I came to my senses, I asked if we had any ketchup left. She pushed up from the table and ambled into the kitchen. I couldn't tell if she seemed slower and stiffer this year compared to last year. I had never seen either of my grandparents ill and must have assumed, on some level, that they would remain just as they were forever.

When she came back with a jar of chutney, she said, "Sometimes it's better not to listen to Dickey," and I nodded. Any hope that she would not apply the chutney herself soon vanished. We couldn't afford to put in electricity, and in any case my grandparents believed refrigeration on the island was a form of corruption. The icebox was really no better than a suitcase with an ice cube inside, and the chutney lived on a shelf where it had grown its own brand of mold, the toxic effects of which Grandma claimed would be inoculated against by the chutney itself.

"Eat," she said, her chin tucked into her chest like a fist shoved into a jacket pocket. "It's not every day you get hamburger for supper."

"I know," I said and felt guilty. I hadn't done anything to deserve it. My grandfather had wanted me to fix a break in the screen door before he came home and help Grandma by cleaning salt off the windows. Also, some of the steps on the back porch had rotted out. I hadn't done anything to help since he'd left with my sister and cousins. When I was halfway through the hamburger, Grandma reached across the table and gently brushed my bangs out of my eyes. She looked worried, and I thought it must be about money.

Earlier in the summer I overheard my grandparents talking in the kitchen about whether they could afford to keep the island house going for the rest of the family, who cycled through from June to September. After raising three children and looking after half-a-dozen grandchildren, my grandparents now had trouble paying the taxes on the house in Vaughn and the house on the island. Both my grandparents had small teachers' pensions from the state but little savings. My father, who had moved in with people he referred to as his "community" over on China Lake, was no help.

After supper, Grandma and I cleaned the dishes. She gave me one of her homemade molasses cookies (my favorite food) that she doled out like pieces of gold on Saturday nights only. We had an hour before we had to head for the airport, so we settled in to read. I was reading *The Secret History of the Special Air Services*, the British SAS, in North Africa during World War II. No one in my family would understand if I told them that my ambition in life was to join the SAS. If I survived the rest of high school, I would sign up. According to the history of the North African campaign, Sir David Stirling, the founder of the SAS, was a friend of the poet Dylan Thomas and carried a copy of his *Twenty-Five Poems* with him through the entire war. My grandfather, a retired English teacher, disparaged Dylan Thomas for some reason, but I understood why Sir David had kept the Welsh bard's words in his breast pocket as he and his men swarmed through the desert in their fleets of attack jeeps. I understood the spirit of the Service, and I clung to the dubious notion that my ability to recite Thomas's poems from memory would compensate for my not being British. But I also worried that I wouldn't have the courage to do what I needed to do in battle. There was a good chance that I would cut and run, like Dickey's ancestor, in order to save my own skin.

When Grandma put down her book and went into the kitchen for two more cookies, one for each of us, I knew something had to be wrong. I told her I had saved $150 from working in the post office and I could give it to her. I had actually saved $175, but I had my eye on a new clock radio.

She picked up her book, licked a finger, and turned a page. "$150," she said eventually. "That's a lot of presents for your girlfriend Charlotte."

"She's not my girlfriend," I said and ate my cookie in the same way she did, by breaking off small pieces and setting them on my knee before placing them in my mouth. When I turned one of the pages of my book, I caught her looking at me.

After dark, Grandma and I met Dickey at the island landing, and we all climbed into the skiff. My mother had only been gone for a couple months, but it seemed to me that she might have changed beyond recognition. I was nervous about meeting her.

Grandma pulled on the starter cord, and the engine coughed but didn't start. I told her to let me try.

"Wait," Dickey said and put a hand on her arm.

"Why?" Grandma said and scowled at Dickey. She gripped my arm and pulled me close.

"She's not coming back, not right now. I tried to warn you," Dickey said in a low voice.

"How did you try to warn us?" Grandma said. "How, exactly? Oh, for God's sake."

"I don't know . . ." he shrugged. "She said she was in love."

Grandma groaned from deep in her chest. "I knew you weren't telling us everything," she said.

"I'm sorry," Dickey said. A minute later she told him it wasn't his fault. I felt a bolt of anger for Dickey, but it didn't last. He hadn't wanted to deliver the bad news.

The hull rocked under us. Across the water, a green light flashed on the black hump of the mainland. Though I wouldn't have said so to Grandma or Dickey, I never wanted to see my mother or hear her voice again. As if I'd spoken my thoughts, they both looked at me, and I wanted to claw back what I felt.

The great blue heron that often rested on the rocks next to the dock spread its wings and leaped into the darkness. We couldn't trace its gray body against the night sky, but we could hear the whoosh of its wings and sense the air displaced by its flight brush the surface of the water. No one could stay aloft forever, not even my mother. I didn't hate her, couldn't afford to.

As we walked across the island in silence, Dickey rested his hand on my shoulder. At Devereux's Field, where the trail split, he lifted his hand and we began to part ways.

"Good night, Dickey," Grandma said.

"Good night, Mrs. H."

When Grandma and I reached the far end of the field, she stumbled in the grass and caught herself. Gripping the air with her fists, she swayed and stared at the gunmetal-blue shadows at the edge of the woods. If I had known then that people do disappear, I would have taken Grandma's arm and held her to me. Instead, I stood by as she breathed deeply. A minute passed, and she started walking toward the house again. I followed a few steps behind her. In the parlor I froze when she froze with her hand on my grandfather's chair.

"I don't care what your mother does; your home is with us now," she said over her shoulder. When she had waited long enough to be sure I had heard, we climbed the stairs. At the top, she turned right, and I turned left. I undressed and climbed under the covers. I knew Grandma had meant what she'd said; I wanted to believe her. Outside my window the moon traced a silver line from the distant islands across the bay to the cove below our house. A breeze filtered through the screen and touched my neck, and I listened to the long, shallow waves collapsing on the beach with a hush.

Make Way for Ducklings
(1990)

John Jacobs Howland

In her caramel jumper and black cap squashed down over frosted hair, my coworker Sharon looked like a burned marshmallow. Her focus ping-ponged over the spot where Jeff, head counselor level two, was supposed to be standing with the keys to the van. As a counselor level one, I was supposed to take the keys from Jeff and, once I had unlocked the van, escort the seven residents out of the building to board the van. In the parking lot, however, no Jeff and no van.

Sharon lit a cigarette and asked Jesus for guidance. She'd been working for five years at the Spurwink House for Boys and Girls, a residential facility run by the state of Maine for children aged six to thirteen who'd been removed from foster homes. Recently, she'd been demoted and put on probation for smoking on the premises and failing to count the knives. Now I counted the knives.

The kids ignored my hand signals to stay in the building. Carla, the oldest at thirteen, and her acolytes, Eric, Tess, Willa and Mitchell, came across the parking lot. All five of them looked at the blank space where the van should've been, took in the no-Jeff situation, and stared at me. It had been my idea to go to the museum. Now we had no Saturday "fun activity."

"Well," Sharon said, squinting philosophically at the sky and the tree line across the road, "we're all here because we're not all there, aren't we? Everyone in my station wagon. I'm fucking driving."

Eric, age nine, set his backpack on the asphalt. "But Jeff would not approve this action!" he said. "And you're not supposed to swear!" He covered the thick lenses of his square glasses with both hands.

"But he's not here, is he? Come on—the will of God will never take you where the grace of God will not protect you," Sharon said and threw open the back of the station wagon.

"Hold on," I said, but the kids followed the strongest leader. Without Jeff they would always gravitate to Sharon's size and the blustering confidence of her AA-isms. The kids crawled through the back into the middle seat. Tess tumbled into the front. Eric hesitated and looked at me with his mouth gaping. I told him to get in the back, and I climbed in after him.

"I don't like it when she swears," he whispered. Sharon rarely swore, and when she did she asked for God's forgiveness, so today we had a different Sharon. She lit a second cigarette from the first. "No smoking!" Eric covered his mouth so he wouldn't catch cancer.

"You think what you're going through is a big deal, Mr. Let Go, Let God," Sharon said to me. Ever since I'd seen Sharon at a meeting on Congress Street, she'd been speaking to me in AA lingo. I saw in the mirror that her hands shook as she pulled onto the road. Also, she closed one eye like someone aiming down the barrel of a rifle.

"There's nothing wrong with you," she said. "Just a small addiction problem for you. Pretty-boy pill popper!"

Sharon was right. In rehab they told me I'd been using illegally acquired pills to cover up my real problems, which doctors would fix with legally acquired pills. I doubted that. In the meantime, I'd been going to AA instead of NA, which overflowed with frightening addicts.

"You'll finish college and meet some girl and get a job and have kids and live in a house with an attached garage."

"What makes you think all that's going to happen?"

"I don't think," Sharon said hoarsely and started coughing.

"I can't breathe!" Carla leaned her head out the window and gulped for air. Sharon rolled her window all the way down, but now the smoke and flaking ash were sucked in through Carla's window and pooled in the back of the station wagon.

"Sharon," Eric said, trying a softer tone, "you're not supposed to smoke. It will make you die."

Though one of the youngest, Eric always had the most to say. Whenever he didn't get the answer he wanted, he forgot to push his bottle glasses up his nose, and his thin, pale nostrils started to twitch like the gills of a trout.

"Shut up back there," Sharon said. I poked my head into the front seat area and noticed that we were driving in the wrong lane. Possibly had been for a few minutes. One of Sharon's eyes looked right at me, but the other one, drooping and wandering, seemed to scan the seat for loose change.

I reached for the wheel, which was when I smelled the whiskey. Sharon veered left. We just missed the edge of a culvert, bumped down from the pavement, rolled slowly across a field, and came to a stop in the furrows of harvested corn.

I had tumbled into the front seat and landed on Tess, age eight. Both she and I seemed unhurt. Tess touched herself all over with her index finger. Eric, laughing and shaking with adrenaline, jumped outside with his backpack worn front forward to protect him from wild dogs.

"There's been a fucking incident! A fucking incident!" he yelled. In the case of an "incident," which this certainly was, we were supposed to call Jeff, though I didn't have a cell phone. Neither did Sharon. It was the early '90s.

"And you promised me pictures in a museum!" Eric aimed his finger at my face and shouted. "Pictures of fucking boats!"

"I know I did," I said, using the calm voice Jeff had taught me. *Use the calm voice like a fire extinguisher.*

"Boats," he moaned.

If we tried to walk to the museum—which we couldn't do, no way, too far—Carla and Eric would wander into traffic or into strange neighborhoods or suddenly, for no reason, climb the side of an embankment and dive headfirst off an overpass. Eric's file, which I was not supposed to have seen at my level, indicated that such things might happen at any moment even if we successfully created a "nurturing home environment" for him. "Just keep them breathing," Jeff said. "That's all we can hope for."

"We're getting out of here," said Carla. "Going to see my boyfriend. He'll drive us anywhere we wanna go." They all marched into the field, headed west. Toward Randolph? They approached the tree line with backs as rigid as flag bearers.

"No!" I said weakly.

Only Eric and Mute Mitchell—*The Mute*, as Sharon called him when Jeff was not around—stood next to me. Older than Eric by a year but smaller, Mitchell clung to the straps of his backpack as if it were a parachute. Unlike some of the other students, Carla and Eric included, Mitchell had never been, according to his file, on suicide watch, but that's what worried me. Mitchell's blank expression and closed mouth defied my ability to form an impression of him. As soon as I closed my eyes, he vanished in my mind.

60

He studied me, then Sharon, and decided to follow Carla. Off he went in the direction of the girls.

"No," I said, but I made no effort to stop him. In extreme circumstances, regulations dictated that I restrain the residents. Wards of the state, they could not be allowed to run away. But knowing about the horrible things that had happened to most of them, I couldn't understand how it was okay for me to touch them at all. Ever.

"Come back," I said. None of them turned around.

Sure that Eric trusted Carla more than me, I feared he would follow the girls and begged him to stay put.

"Are they coming back?" Eric asked. In addition to dog attacks, he feared that the counselors and other residents would leave him, and he had good reason to be afraid. Counselors, especially level ones earning minimum wage, frequently vanished. Sharon had worked there the longest. Jeff, the head counselor, had been there for two years, and he'd recently told me that after another year, when his girlfriend finished nursing school, they planned to move to Boston. Residents, too, would suddenly take off, sometimes back to foster care, but often to the Mercy psych unit or to juvenile detention.

On the far side of the field, four small heads, one blond, one red, two brown, ducked into the trees.

"Shit," I said. I wasn't upset, not yet. I never really felt things while they were happening. Always sometime later.

"I should've followed them," Eric said. "Now they're gone and I'm not."

"I'm here, so is Sharon," I said, though Sharon was unconscious and drooling on the steering wheel.

"Is she dead?" Eric asked.

"I don't think so." I looked more closely. She was breathing. I knew I should probably edge over to check.

Eric leapt into Sharon's lap and started to dig around in the glove compartment until he found a Snickers, which he carefully unwrapped and fumbled onto the floor. When he dove under Sharon's legs to root out the Snickers from amidst cigarette butts and the remains of an Egg McMuffin, his upturned sneakers pushed against Sharon's slack jaw and mashed her nose against her face.

"She has the hungry disease," Eric shouted back to me. Sharon was diabetic, but I could smell whiskey. She had to be passed out drunk. Snickers in hand, Eric pried open Sharon's mouth, used his finger to push her tongue out of the way, and jammed the Snickers a little too far down Sharon's throat. Gripping the top of her forehead with one hand and her jaw with the other, he started to manually masticate the candy bar for her.

"Stop, that's not going to work," I said half-heartedly. I supposed a Snickers couldn't hurt Sharon unless she started to choke. Sharon wasn't my biggest worry. All but one resident had disappeared into the Maine woods. For that I might get more than fired.

"Yes, it will work!" Eric said. A film of sweat pooled on his brow and chin. Satisfied, he gently rested Sharon's face against the steering wheel. Chocolate oozed out of her mouth. Maybe if I didn't do something she might choke, but then I saw several gooey chunks slide down into her lap. Bubbles appeared on her lips. The will to live.

"Now what?" Eric demanded. "Are we just going to leave her here?" His mouth opened wide with shock. "What if someone comes and puts dirt in her mouth?"

"You already basically did that."

"What if a pack of dogs come along and tries to eat her!" His pupils dilated, his breathing grew shallow, and he started to scan the edges of the field.

"We'll call for help from the house," I said, trying to sound calm, and grabbed his hand. What I really needed was for someone to lead me back to the house—I had just lost a whole houseful of kids. My breath grew shallow and my vision started to narrow.

"How far back to the home?" Eric asked. The shrinks who visited the kids for a few minutes once a week wanted them to call the building "home."

"Maybe a mile."

"A mile!" He gawked at me. "We can't walk a mile. We need to take a ride. Where the fuck is Jeff!"

"Good question. Come on. It's not going to kill you to walk a mile." Now that I had his hand, I wasn't going to let him go.

Eric squinted at the sky. The morning haze had turned the sky the color of chicken skin. "I don't want to die," he moaned and slowly sat in the breakdown lane with one hand draped over his brow and his other gripping my hand.

"You're not going to die," I said.

"But that's not true. You know that's not true. I *am* going to die."

"I mean not today," I said.

"Can you promise that?"

"No," I said. We had a pact not to lie to each other. Eric had established the pact, and I had agreed because it was easier at first to go along.

"Then why did you say 'not today'?"

"To calm you down."

"But now I am less calm."

"That's because you don't want to be calm."

"But yes I do!" he said and widened his eyes. "I want to be calm. And I thought we were going to the museum. To see the paintings of boats, the most beautiful paintings of boats I'd ever seen, you said."

"We are—I mean we were."

"But then Sharon drove us into the field."

"That's what happened, yes." I took a deep breath. "I don't think we should tell Jeff about what happened today." Immediately I regretted what I had said. Not telling Jeff wouldn't bring the kids back, wouldn't protect them wherever they were. And now I had asked Eric to lie. Eric never lied. Whatever passed through his head came right out of his mouth—this was in his file—so it was not fair to ask him to hide the truth. To cover my motives, I said, "If we tell, Sharon might get in trouble—she'll get fired." Then I felt even worse because for all I knew we had left Sharon to drown in her own spittle.

"Who will read *Make Way for Ducklings*?" Eric demanded.

I hadn't thought of this problem. A serious problem. Sharon had to be the one to read. It didn't say so in Eric's file, but it was the case. Each resident had two stories, the one in their file and the one not in their file. The one you could read in one sitting that seemed to explain everything about them and the other one that only flickered, as it did now from the corner of Eric's mouth. I helped him to his feet and lifted his backpack onto his shoulders. I told him it wasn't far. He cringed with each footfall, and with every step he rose on the ball of his right foot and pitched forward slightly because his right toe was missing.

We walked for a minute, sat down to take a rest, and walked for another minute. With its white clapboards and black shutters, the Spurwink House looked like a home where a family might live. Inside, though, the second floor had been divided into seven tiny rooms; downstairs, padlocks secured the drawers and the refrigerator. Only four months out of Mercy rehab myself and only three months on the job, I had keys to the place. Why had someone given me the keys? Look what had happened.

Eric checked all the windows, which remained locked day and night for the safety of the residents. I sat down on the sofa to worry about the escapees. I had signed a stack of papers when I took the job, but I hadn't read any of them. Maybe they could sue me. Put me in jail.

Eric lay down parallel to me on the floor.

"Am I tired now?" he said. "A bit sleepy?"

I had said to him once that he didn't seem to realize when he was tired or hungry. He would go and go, then just drop.

"You are," I said. I was usually tired, too, especially during the day.

"When are you leaving?" he asked.

"I didn't say I was leaving."

"Everyone leaves."

His fears orbited his thoughts, returning with regularity.

A message beeped on the answering machine next to the phone. Leaning up from the sofa, I pushed the play button. Jeff coughed out of the speaker. He had the flu and had slept through his alarm. We should brave the museum without him, go ahead and take the van. Oh, but, shit, he said, I have the van.

Now that we'd had an "incident," I should call Jeff, but with Jeff out of action, technically I should call Terry, the administrator in charge of the house. Despite his soft name and scratchy-looking therapist-beard, Terry was scary. He judged with his ripsaw green eyes and kept files on all the employees. The first question he asked me in our interview was "John, do you like to have sex with children?" "No!" I might have answered too loudly but got the job anyway, possibly only because my grandmother knew his boss. Terry's emergency phone number hung on the wall above the phone and seemed to pulse in my vision. If something terrible happened to just *one* of the children out there—and something terrible had already happened to each of them; that's why they were here at the Spurwink House with no one but me in charge—Terry would put me in the same category as the people who'd damaged these kids to begin with. I would have to stand trial.

"I don't think we should call Terry right away," I said.

"Don't call Terry!" Eric said. Most of the residents hated Terry.

The phone rang, and Eric shot across the room to grab the receiver and bring it to me. Jeff, wanting a status update. He had spent the morning puking his guts out.

"No museum," I reported.

"Yeah, I will be there as soon as I can. Keep everyone calm and in the house until I get there?"

"Okay," I said, "will do."

"Did you just lie?" Eric asked when I hung up. He stood only a foot away from my face.

"Yes, but not to you."

He furrowed his brow and evaluated this statement as he rested his hand on top of my head.

"Okay, but who is going to read *Make Way for Ducklings* tonight?"

If Sharon did not read *Make Way for Ducklings*—and it had to be Sharon—Eric would destroy his room.

"I can read it," I said.

"No," he said and grimaced.

The rules for handling each resident depended on their file. No Vicks VapoRub around Eric, no dogs around Denise (or Eric), do not say the name Doug around Stephanie, no loose buttons around Mitchell. The smell of tuna fish made Willa throw up. Don't let Carla use the phone to call her boyfriend because her boyfriend only existed in the back of the 1983 *National Geographic*, which featured a racecar driver named Craig Dempsey. Eric grew up in Mexico, Maine, with his mother and her boyfriends in an old farmhouse with no running water, no electricity. Half the time she didn't come home for days at a time. The last boyfriend, a homebody, sodomized Eric with Vicks VapoRub and kept him locked in a closet in his own piss and shit until he almost died. Eric ran away through the woods in the middle of the winter with nothing but socks on his feet, which explained his missing toe but not the pale, oval-shaped scar on his forehead or the scars on his back.

Nothing had ever happened to me. In Tucson I drank too much, took too many pills and other things. Then one day I stopped eating, stopped sleeping, stopped talking. Everything stopped. It felt as if my brain was suspended in black Jell-O. My roommate's girlfriend found me in my bedroom on the floor, my lips blue. At first I told people in the hospital that I hadn't known the stuff was cut—*Apache*. When I landed back at University Med a month later, I admitted I knew what I was doing, and they locked me down for seventy-two hours. During an interview with one of the doctors, I said that my mother had left us when I was fourteen. I'd hardly seen her since. The doctor asked me if I thought that might have something to do with what had been happening to me. I didn't know, I told the doctor—maybe.

I was back in Maine now because my grandmother had come out to Tucson to see me for the third time, this time to bring me back for good, and I was still here in Maine because she was still alive. On my days off I drove north to spend the night at my grandparents' house, where my grandmother sometimes told me she was happy to see me getting better. But I wasn't getting better. I didn't believe anyone changed, not at this point in my life. People kept going as long as they could. Then they didn't.

Eric stood above me, squinting at the side of my face. Something I wished he wouldn't do. I had nothing to offer him. I told him to take out his colored pencils and a drawing pad and spread them next to the sofa. Eric needed special permission to use his colored pencils. He always drew the same lobster boat with a black hull under a yellow sky. No people, no land, no gulls.

"Is this good enough to be in the museum?" he asked, turning the drawing so I could see the black hull sitting in the white water.

"If I were in charge of the museum, I would put it right in the front." I wasn't lying, and he knew it. He nodded thoughtfully.

"Look!" Eric pointed across the road to where Mitchell stood on the shoulder with his hands hanging at his sides. "He came back!"

Mitchell stood as steady as a lamppost and showed no sign that he planned to cross the road on his own, thank God. Though he'd never said he hated the Spurwink House, he had drawn me a crude picture of a building under which he'd written, "I hate hate hate it hear." At the time I had wondered if he meant he hated (it?) here or what he once had to hear.

I opened the door. "Mitchell, stay where you are!"

Something moved in the woods behind Mitchell, and in moments Carla and the others appeared. I told Eric to wait for me, but he burst into the middle of the road without looking either way and held out his palms, one facing each direction. Mitchell extended his foot, careful not to touch the white line, and marched toward me. Carla and the others caught up to him and slinked across the road.

"Make way for the fucking ducklings!" Eric shouted down the empty road.

I'd almost herded them inside when I saw Sharon crossing the road with her hands gripping the top of her head as if it might fall off. Inside, Sharon lay down on the sofa and Carla flopped down on the floor in the middle of the room and sighed. In obedience to their leader, the others did the same.

"No one, I mean no one, is allowed to leave the building under any circumstances," I said in my best Terry voice, but no one paid attention to me. I tried to count them to make sure we had everyone, but I kept losing count. Unable to remember how many there were supposed to be, I sat down and yawned. When I slept at night I didn't really sleep, and when I was awake during the day I wasn't really awake.

"You find your boyfriend?" Eric asked Carla.

"Shut up, Eric," Carla said. Eric crawled over and put his head on Carla's stomach. Without exception, the residents were not allowed to touch each other.

"Sharon, why did you pass out?" Eric asked.

"Hah, hah, hah," Sharon laughed. "That's the funny part! I wasn't drunk at all—but for the grace of God. Do you know what I mean? You will. I ate a cookie for breakfast, which for me is ten times as bad as drinking five gallons of Ballantine. But not really!" She laughed again. "Why would I eat a cookie when I know what it does to me? And then you know what happened? Instead of dying, this urchin Eric came along and with his little fingers placed a piece of Snickers on my tongue. A miracle! I was there but also not there, you know? I had one foot in this troubled world and one foot out. Old Sharon here was floating over the hood of the car watching you all, and I saw John there shaking his head. And Carla and Mitchell walking off—you were not alone! I was watching over you. And seeing I could not chew for myself, seeing I had already given up on the flesh, my cherub here put the Snickers in my mouth and started *chewing for me* using his little hands. I saw all this from above, you understand, and even though I had already let go, let God, even though I had already surrendered the shit out of this situation and all future situations, if you know what I mean, all things, even my own thoughts, needing to be accepted as things I could not control, my heart just swelled with my Higher Power at the sight of Eric chewing for his big old Sharon. And that's when I decided that I couldn't, God willing, leave you guys alone down here."

Sharon broke off, breathless, and taking Eric in her thick arms lifted him off the floor and danced around the room with his legs dangling unhinged from his hips. When she set him down, Eric collapsed, giggling as if Sharon had been tickling him.

Sharon fell half on, half off the sofa and leaned her head back, mouth open. Eric crawled onto Sharon's lap and closed his eyes. No one had eaten lunch, and it would be suppertime soon. Because of people's medication schedules and general sensitivity to blood sugar fluctuations, there were no exceptions to mealtimes. The plan had been to hand out bag lunches at the museum courtyard, but lunch did not exist because Jeff had been in charge of lunch.

"Should we read *Make Way for Ducklings* now?" Sharon asked. "I feel like reading it now."

"But we always read it after supper." Eric seemed genuinely concerned about what would happen after supper, or maybe if supper would even happen ever again.

"Let's read it now *and* after supper," Sharon said.

They all looked to me.

"Today," Sharon finally said as she held up her hand for someone to fetch *Ducklings*, "I was saved by my Higher Power, who proved to me—as if he needed to!—that He is always looking out for me. Always! And each one of you has Higher Powers of your own understanding, and these Higher Powers are all looking out for you. You will never be given more than you can handle."

Eric pulled the flop-eared copy out of the drawer where we kept the board games and solemnly handed it to Sharon. Everyone settled on the floor and stared off at the walls.

"*Mr. and Mrs. Mallard were looking for a place to live. But every time Mr. Mallard saw what looked like a nice place, Mrs. Mallard said it was no good . . . she was not going to raise a family where there might be foxes or turtles.*" They had all heard the story hundreds of times by now, and most of them were too old for it, but within three sentences all their eyes glazed over with an opiatic haze. Eric fell sound asleep as the new ducklings, Jack, Kack, Lack, Mack, Nack, Quack, and Pack, passed the corner shop on Charles Street. In the Public Garden, where they almost got run over by a kid on a bike, and were snubbed by a giant haughty swan on a paddle boat, Mrs. Mallard said she would not raise ducklings in such a violent place. So they moved to an island in the middle of the Charles River. That was fine—made sense, but then *Mr. Mallard decided he'd like to take a trip to see what the rest of the river was like, farther on. So off he set.* So off he set? They agreed to meet a week (a week!) later in the Public Garden. "*Don't you worry,*" said Mr. Mallard. Where in the Public Garden exactly would they meet? Having been there myself, I didn't see how you could just decide to meet a duck somewhere in the park. And how would they get there? The ducklings only had to travel a thousand feet at most from the Esplanade to the northwest corner of the park, but they had to pass over Back Street or Beaver Place and busy Beacon Street, where the friendly cop named Michael came along to stop traffic for them. Even with the help of the cops, only a miracle could explain the absence of fatalities by car, cat, shoe, or seagull. They marched across the park to the pond and there found the vacationing Mr. Mallard relaxing and waiting for them to arrive. They had landed here in the beginning of the book and had found too many reckless kids on bikes and the paddle boat with the strange aloof swan—the same place about which Mrs. Mallard had said, "*This is no place for babies.*" Now she thought, *I'm okay with it?*

On a normal day, the last line of the story would send Eric off to bed, and he would crawl under the sheets and close his eyes. A normal day ended after supper at 7:45. The current time, 4:30, left him with three hours and fifteen minutes that he couldn't account for or work around. I saw him try. I spoke to him in my thoughts and told him to breathe, just breathe—another valuable piece of advice from Jeff that usually didn't work. Eric leaned forward, placed his hands on both sides of his head, and squeezed with his eyes closed and his mouth open. Maybe if Sharon continuously reread the story from now until 7:45, he would then close his eyes and heave a sigh of relief.

"Eric," I said, but he didn't hear me. When he finally raised his head, glasses perched on the end of his nose, nostrils flaring, he looked right through me. I said his name again, but he didn't respond. He rose slowly to his feet and, slouching like a kid off to do his chores, climbed the stairs to his room. I followed him, and the rest of the kids followed me. He swung the door open, grabbed the end of the blanket on his bed, and slowly pulled it onto the floor. He leaned forward, and for a moment it seemed as if he might be too tired to continue. The other kids pressed behind me to gain a better view. Downstairs the microwave hummed—Sharon making herself a snack. Eric grabbed his cover, yanked it across the room, then swept his hands across his bookshelf. Matchbox cars, books, and drawing materials flew onto the floor. He tipped over the bookshelf, ripped a poster of a racecar Jeff had just bought him off the wall, and frantically tore it into small pieces. Picking up speed, he pulled out the drawers, dragged them across the room, and dumped them upside down. His underwear, T-shirts, and pants landed in a pile. He leaned his shoulder into the bureau and pushed it over. A clay cup he had painted broke. A plastic sailboat I'd bought for him cracked. His glasses flew off his face as he screamed and pounded his fists into the wall. I called his name, but he didn't seem to hear me. Every other time Eric had spun out, Jeff had been here to restrain him with the bearhug move they had taught us in training. A move reserved for moments when we thought residents might hurt themselves—moments like this. But I stood staring at Eric as he swung his fist as hard as he could and left a bloody mark on the plaster. He looked over his shoulder at me and tightened his fist for a second shot. Jeff would already have tackled him by now.

"Don't, Eric. Please."

But he did anyway—of course he did—because I hadn't stopped him. His fist slammed into the same spot as if driven by a force of its own, and without thinking I pinned him to the floor, clamped his arms to his sides, and squeezed his legs together with my knees. Spit flew from his mouth as he growled and tried to twist his head around to bite me.

"Breathe," I told him because he was starting to hyperventilate. His ribs pounded against my arms. "Breathe, Eric," I whispered. When he heard his name a second time, he opened his bloodshot eyes and looked at me. He recognized me. He looked around his room, at the bare walls and broken toys. While I waited for him to calm, he rested his head against my arm and stared up at my face.

"You ready to get up?" I asked after a while. He didn't answer at first. His warm breath washed over my cheeks.

"Yeah," he said.

The other kids had lost interest and gone downstairs. I took one end of his sheet, and he took the other. I pushed the bookshelf back against the wall, and he placed the pieces of the broken cup and shattered sailboat back on the shelf. The poster had been shredded; we scooped the scraps into his wastebasket.

When we finished, he sat on the edge of the mattress and hunched his shoulders. I sat next to him.

"I'm tired," he said.

"I am, too," I said. I asked him if he felt ready to eat, and he nodded. Jeff would arrive anytime and hand out everyone's medication, and then it would be time for me to go home and eat. I started to walk out of his room, but he told me to wait.

"What is it?"

"You're leaving."

"In a few minutes, I'm just going home for the night. Jeff is coming in, and so is Sandra. It's the same every week. I'll be back in the morning." So yes, I wanted to say to him—I needed to leave—and not just because I was starving and my hands were shaking. Now I was feeling what I hadn't felt before: the panic of watching the kids walk across the field away from me. Whatever happened to them would be my fault.

For a moment, as Eric removed his glasses and cleaned them on his T-shirt, he looked like an old man. He replaced his glasses on his face and stood waiting for me to lead the way downstairs.

Sandra arrived first, relieving Sharon, who took a cab home. When Jeff pulled into the parking lot soon afterward, I decided not to mention our trip in Sharon's station wagon. His stomach still felt weak, he said, but he'd survive the night. Sandra would sit between the bedrooms upstairs while Jeff counted the knives after supper and tried to sleep on the sofa. I waved goodnight to everyone and ran across the parking lot to the Datsun my grandmother had lent me.

I lived half an hour away in Portland in the back of a third-story three-bedroom walkthrough with two other guys from AA I didn't know too well. My one bedroom window overlooked a parking lot and a 7-Eleven. I couldn't wait to get to the apartment and not talk to anyone.

In the kitchen, I heated toast in the oven and sipped from a glass of water. The other two guys hadn't come home yet. So tired that I felt as if I had sand in my eyes, I pushed the toast aside and rested my forehead on the table. The phone rang, and when

I picked up the receiver, a voice on the other end said, "John?" I recognized him right away.

"How'd you get this number, Eric?" He didn't answer. He must've somehow broken into the office while Jeff slept. Sandra must've fallen asleep, too. I pictured the house—dark, locked, and quiet except for Eric's whisper.

"Is everything all right?" Eric asked.

"With me?"

He said that I'd seemed upset when I left. Troubled. He parroted the language of his doctors and social workers, but not with irony—he wanted to help. The answer to his question was that I was not all right, not at all. I had no idea how I had ended up like this and no idea what to do about it.

"When are you going to leave?" he asked.

"I'm coming back tomorrow. Remember, I told you."

"You're going to leave," he said. I told him he was just feeling anxious—I would see him in the morning. But I wouldn't see him in the morning. I would call in sick, and on the day after that I wouldn't bother to call. I just wouldn't show up. To be certain of all that would never happen to me—I'd yet to stick a needle in my arm, yet to spend a night in jail—I needed to forget the Spurwink House.

"You promise?" Eric said, and I promised him.

I hung up and went to our kitchen window, which overlooked the roof of the bar next door and, at the end of the block, Longfellow Square. Often a man stood below Longfellow's statue and hurled warnings about the Second Coming at passing traffic. Tonight he sat leaning against the poet's leg with his head in his hands. I'd seen him at the same AA meeting where I'd seen Sharon, but I couldn't remember his name. Couldn't remember his story. I could only remember his voice in the parking lot after the meeting asking one person after another if they could give him a ride home.

Flood
(1992)

Franklin Mitchell, Betty Howland Mirack,
Mainwaring Hayes Howland

Residents of fifty homes in Vaughn were evacuated after heavy rains and melting snow caused the Kennebec River to overflow its banks. Several families trapped by rising water had to be rescued. State wardens used a boat to save a pack of hunting dogs from their kennel, and one man had to be ferried back to his home because he had fled without taking any money with him. The largest single evacuation took place at the Victorian Villa Rehabilitation and Living Center on Pleasant Street, a nursing home and residential care facility for seniors. Dairy farmers moved their cows to higher ground. The waters flooded a potato farm and warehouses and submerged cars and trucks. Volunteer firefighters moved all their firefighting apparatus to the town garage before floodwater encircled the fire station. Most roads leading in and out of town were shut down. Some families took shelter in the American Legion Hall, where children whooped and watched television. Maine Emergency Management Agency officials flew over Vaughn in a Forest Service helicopter. They also took photographs.

When Franklin saw the water cross the street and flow toward his shop, Vaughn Antiques, he and his friend Mainwaring started moving things to the apartment upstairs. They took the larger items first, the sea trunks, chests, a pew from the old United Church, a loveseat, a wing chair. Mainwaring left to see if his great-aunt Betty needed any help, and Franklin carried the other things (hooked rugs, Wedgwood, a series of old electric clocks, farm tools, old lamps, rum casks, books) and stacked them in careful piles on the cracked linoleum of his second-story kitchen and on the old shag carpeting of the bedroom. The postcard collection and Rogers silver he placed on top of the dresser. On the quilt he set the delicate musical instruments, a violin, clarinet, and cello, all of them dilapidated and beyond repair. The oil-lamp globes he rested on the various straight-backed chairs, one for each seat. The most important items, the globes and the instruments, were not, by far, the most valuable. He also did not want to lose his collection of tintypes, which included a six-fingered Union soldier holding a banjo. After he finished arranging everything, he stood back. All his things looked so out of place stacked on the carpet and chairs. The flood wouldn't last long, he told himself, but there was no way of knowing exactly how long.

He restacked the books on the floor, moving them away from the window in case any dampness came through, and he rewrapped the glass lampshades in tissue paper to prevent any chipping when he moved them back downstairs. Nothing made him feel better, though. Everything was out of place. He checked the shop once more, opening the front door so the water wouldn't break in, and went back upstairs to sit on the rug amidst his things and wait.

The river continued to rise past dark. The electricity went out; the phone went dead. Outside, the streetlamps hung like the limbs of winter hardwoods. The water lapped the walls downstairs, and the current rushed along the cobbled walkways, heading south toward Gardner, Dresden Mills, and the ocean.

In the morning, Dom's station wagon sat in front of his barbershop, the water halfway up the wheels. Dom stood in the window of the second story looking at the street. Franklin waved, but Dom didn't see. Though only the last week of February, the air had warmed enough for Franklin to take off the argyle sweater his mother had given him for Christmas and fold it over the silver platter he had bought from old Mrs. Ellis after her husband died. She had told him the silver came from her husband's family, along with his old wing chair and a silver-tipped cane. Mrs. Ellis, from Bangor, had no children, and she didn't like any of her husband's relatives, who all lived in Augusta. She didn't want any of them to have her husband's things. "Better they go to strangers," she said. Mrs. Ellis lived in a small room in a giant unheated house, and her one luxury was canned fruit on Sunday night.

Franklin started a fire in the kitchen stove and put a can of soup on top. Only a matter of time now, he thought, and sure enough, by afternoon he could walk out the front door into the street. His shop remained untouched except for banks of mud against the baseboards and layers of silt over the wood floors, which wouldn't warp any more than they already had. His mother would worry about the smell (she owned the building), but no matter how many times he scrubbed, it would be August before the mildew vanished. The basement would be a full six feet underwater, and it would take a sump pump to fix the problem. Outside, branches, piles of mud, bald tires, and trash covered the sidewalks and road. Two telephone poles canted toward each other, the wires like a black smile across the silver sky.

Other people who owned shops on Water Street—the Boyntons, Mr. Dawson, Tom from Tom's Pizza, and old Johnson, who owned the Wilson's—came down from their houses on the hill and looked in the windows of their stores. Panes were busted or cracked, but the water had never come close to the notch on the granite corner of the Hay Building that marked the 1885 flood, which had poured through the front doors of the Methodist Church on Second Street. It could have been much worse. The men hired to plow in the winter joined the VFD in cleaning up the downtown. They arrived with chainsaws to buck up whole trees that had floated down the street and gathered in the parking lot of the Gardner Savings Bank.

Franklin helped Mr. and Mrs. Boynton clean up the glass and debris in the aisles of their store. Spruce limbs littered the meat counter. An old shoe sat on the bread shelf, and an article of women's underwear had come to rest behind the counter. Mr. Boynton carried it on the end of a stick to a trash bag.

"I feel bad for those people down on River Road," Mrs. Boynton kept saying. "We should do something for them."

Several families from River Road couldn't go back to their homes. They would stay at the Legion while the fire chief talked to people in Augusta about obtaining funds to repair their houses, one of which had pitched forward off its stilts into the mud.

Franklin mopped and scrubbed the first floor of his shop, disinfecting everything before setting up the dehumidifier. He moved his things back downstairs and spent half a day placing everything where it had been, the lamps on one side on a drop-leaf table, the china in an old cupboard he had taken out of a house in Sheepscot. He arranged his leather account book on the ink blotter and rehung the pictures on their wire hangers—the three along the south wall that were conspicuously noted as not being for sale: pictures of his great-grandparents. In their day, this shop had been a store. In the front window, he set up the silver platter and the leather-bound edition of *Old Vaughn Days*, signed by the author in 1888.

A number of people—the Boyntons, the Michauds—stopped by the shop to see how he was getting along after the flood. Everyone in town knew he had had problems when he was young, and not the kind of problem most high school kids have, out at the pit or at keggers in the woods. His mother, a single parent, worked long hours as a nurse at the hospital. Starting in middle school, he often left in the middle of class and walked home. Halfway through high school he dropped out completely.

Franklin knew people thought it strange that his best friends were three times his age—Mrs. Ellis, Mrs. Mirack—Betty—and Mrs. Nason. He was friends with Mainwaring Howland—Betty's nephew—and his wife, both of them young, but only because Mainwaring was related to Betty, his favorite person in town. Franklin knew people said he must be gay; after Allison, he never went out with girls. They called him strange, queer, something wrong with him from the beginning, something mental that couldn't be fixed and that someday might wind him up in the Augusta Mental Health Institute. He knew the way he seemed to people. Almost seven feet tall, his eyes twitched when he talked, his hair had turned prematurely gray and his skin brittle in his mid twenties. He couldn't look people in the face, he hunched like an old man, he smelled like an old man, his hands often shook, and he had trouble wrapping his tongue around words starting with the letter S. He wore the same faded plaid shirt every day. When he was a teenager he started collecting what most people considered junk, and a number of people in Vaughn—all the good people, Betty said—were glad to see him making a go of it, walking down the street with the small leather case he sometimes carried to the bank.

After he finished rearranging the shop, Franklin sat down at his desk. Aside from the smell of mildew, it seemed as if the flood had never happened. He looked out the window. Owners moved through their shops, and people went about their business on the sidewalks. Those people whose houses had been damaged by the flood would have to move in with relatives for a while, and Franklin felt bad for them, but for the rest of Vaughn, the rising water had been nothing more than an inconvenience. They called it an emergency: a bridge in Dresden had gone out; there would be expenses. Help would arrive, though, and after a short time most people would forget.

Several people walking by looked in his window but did not wave. Franklin lifted his hand anyway, palm out in the direction of the window. When he lowered his hand, the skin pulled tightly across his bony knuckles, pale and freckled and dried in a fan of cracks that stretched across the tendons.

He heard a slapping sound out front and went to the door. The Boyntons' grandson, Malcolm, from their youngest daughter Emma, ran from puddle to puddle in the street and stomped his feet until the water drained.

"Malcolm!" Franklin called out, and Malcolm turned and froze. Franklin didn't know why he had yelled. He didn't want to speak to Malcolm—and he didn't care if he stomped in the puddles. Malcolm stared at him for a moment and then resumed his stomping. The water fanned out and glinted in the sharp light.

Back at his desk, Franklin fell asleep only to awaken later in the afternoon grasping his ledger book. In a dream he had seen an unfamiliar iron bridge. He thought nothing of it for the rest of the day and evening until he awoke in the middle of the night with the same image in his head. Just a bridge, surrounded by woods, but he could see every detail of the rusting iron supports and trusses. The stream underneath ran over round white stones the size of apples. For a minute, maybe longer, he couldn't breathe at all. Then he felt calmer. After making himself a cup of tea, he took a shower.

The fire hall auction, scheduled for the day the flood hit, had been rescheduled to begin at nine this morning. Larry Bunker, the VFD treasurer and auctioneer, needed to leave that afternoon for his daughter's house in Millinocket and wouldn't be back for a month. Otherwise, the committee would have put off the auction for another week. A new sign said the proceeds would be donated to help with the flood.

Franklin planned to visit Mainwaring's great-aunt Betty later that morning to see if she needed anything. First, he wanted to look over the items up for bid at the auction. The year before, he'd bought an old refrigerator from the 1940s, but mostly he looked for small things: eyeglasses, gloves, scarves, buttons, things most people had no use for. His favorite finds were old family photographs and pictures of river drives from the 1930s. He never understood why people would get rid of their own family pictures, and every sale of an old photo to a stranger felt like a betrayal of the original owners. Most of the things in his shop came from the houses of people in town, many of them friends of Betty Mirack, who came from one of the oldest families in town through her grandmother's people, the Howlands. Betty's middle name was Howland, but the Miracks and Betty's father's people had worked in the woods. At her house, which she had inherited from her Howland grandmother, Franklin's heart always raced as he passed his hand over tea sets and chairs brought from the Far East by a seafaring ancestor. He always told her not to sell anything—not to him, not to anyone.

At the VFW, where the auction had been moved because of flood damage to the fire hall, he found a water-warped trunk with wallpaper peeling off the inside compartment, a pair of old cracked wooden cross-country skis with one bamboo pole, a velour perfume case filled with assorted buttons, a mustard-colored glass lampshade, a pair of worsted wool hunting pants, a thirty-year-old vacuum cleaner with no hose. He looked through a pile of hand tools, none of them antiques: a rusted shovel with a cracked handle, chisels, screwdrivers, augers. Amidst this junk, however, he spotted a long pole with an iron hook and spike attached to the end, a tool used in log driving—a peavey—and on the neck someone had carved the initials "HC." He rested the pole against the wall and sat in one of the metal chairs in the back row. Twenty or so people, most of them elderly women, made their way to the other seats.

Albert Bunker, Larry's older brother, handed Larry a small box. "We will start the bidding," he said, "with—well, I don't know what this is."

"It's a fondue maker," Albert announced.

"A fondue maker," Larry repeated. He opened the top of the box and rooted around inside. "All the parts seem to be here," he said. "What say we start out at a dollar. Do I have a dollar?" No one bid a dollar. He lowered the bid to fifty cents and twenty- five cents until finally he announced they would come back to the fondue maker after people let themselves warm up. Bidding started on a relatively new chain for a chainsaw. Again no bidders.

"Come on, now," Larry complained. "This would cost you seven dollars new."

Eventually, his brother Albert bid fifty cents and won the chainsaw chain. It took over an hour to reach the peavey that Franklin had found among the tools. He couldn't know for certain that HC stood for Harry Clough, his grandfather, but he bid up to five dollars and fifty cents and won against one of the ladies in the front row. They all turned around to look at him as he walked down for his item.

"I sure hope that stick is worth it," one of them said as he paid Albert. He went out to the parking lot, where he stared at the initials, sure now that the owner of the peavey was his grandfather, who almost exactly a year ago had shot himself in his truck way out on the Blake Road.

A bunch of middle school kids playing on the other side of the street stopped when they saw him and went silent, trying to look away. One of this same bunch had tossed a stone at him back in the fall, bouncing it off the hood of his truck in the parking lot beside Boynton's. When he had walked toward them that night, the tallest one, a MacDonald kid, had called him a fag, and they had all scattered into the shadows. Now, in the daylight, they waited for what he would do. When he ignored them, they resumed their game, a stick battle of some kind.

He no longer felt like visiting Betty. He couldn't get the dream image of the bridge out of his mind. Somehow seeing the kids had pushed it to the front of his thoughts. He had never been bothered by his dreams before. His mother spoke of people in the hospital telling her of their terrifying nightmares—of being chased and strangled and drowned—and some spent hours obsessing over certain fleeting images: a sibling without a face, an ex-wife wearing a top hat. He had always thought such preoccupations reserved for people like many of his customers who drove up from Massachusetts—self-indulgent people.

He stared at the side of his old Ford truck and knew it belonged to him, but it also seemed unfamiliar and distant from his experience. He leaned the peavey against the cab and stood back. A tool, he knew, for moving logs, nothing more. Thousands like it out there.

The early mud season had sent streams of brown water flowing down the valley. He drove around the frost heaves in Central Street on his way to Betty's house, one of the large old Federals on the hill above the river. Her husband had died fifteen years ago, and now, like Mrs. Ellis, she slept in the kitchen on a cot. Betty pulled open the heavy door with two hands and stood smiling, forcing her back erect.

"Yes," she said even though he hadn't asked her anything.

Franklin usually stopped by to visit her once a week. Though the same could be said of many people in town, Betty was a distant relative, distant enough not to be considered a relative at all.

Mr. Mirack's war medals hung in a frame in the front hallway next to an old pine blanket chest and a pedestal table with a porcelain tray and a pair of white leather gloves cast there to harden in place like animal skins. The plaster walls had cracked in wide fissures, the ceiling sagged, the joists bowed. The disrepair of the house and of Betty didn't bother him—he would not have changed anything about the house or her—but he couldn't stand the idea that the decay would grow worse until nothing remained. Whenever he visited her, the feeling of wanting time to stop overwhelmed him.

She waved him in and walked out the back door of the kitchen, where a wall of spruce bordered a half-acre field. An overweight mutt rose to its feet as she approached and bent over its gray muzzle. Franklin sat down at the kitchen table opposite her iron bed, kerosene heater, and black-and-white TV sitting on a Windsor chair. Most things in the house dated from the time of its construction just after the Revolution. Franklin hadn't known any of the history of the area until he'd started collecting and going through his mother's attic, where he discovered and pieced together his own history and the history of the little land his mother still owned around the house.

The armrest of the rocker where he sat had been worn down to the grain by a lifetime of someone rubbing the heel of a hand against the momentum of the chair's sway. Above the chair hung an oil portrait, probably from the early 1800s. After the death of the pictured patriarch, the end of the ice trade and the building of the railroad would have meant the end of the Howlands' good fortune, and the end of the fortunes of the town itself. No one needed the river. Not even for driving pulp.

Betty returned and set the tea out on the kitchen table, pushing the sugar across to him. "Now, Franklin, I know you will be upset with me, but I aim to sell whatever I can. I warned you several times I wanted to talk about this."

"I just came by to see if you were okay after the flood. I know Mainwaring came by, but I wanted to check to see if you needed anything."

"I appreciate that, Franklin, but I was hoping we could talk business."

"I can't buy all the things in your house. I can't afford to."

"You can find someone, though, someone from Portland, maybe, I know you can, to come in and sell it off."

"Yes, ma'am, but what about your son?"

"I've told you Douglas doesn't care. He lives in Illinois with his wife and kids in a big modern house. He doesn't care about these old things. Young people don't care anymore—except you—and why should they? Not even my nephew Mainwaring really cares, you know that. My son Douglas, he's a teacher, his wife works at the police station, and they have four kids who all need things— lessons, summer camps. I can sell these things and give them some of the money, you know. I know you don't approve, Franklin."

"That's not it, but I wish you didn't have to," he said.

"Your father liked old things, too," she said, "but you wouldn't remember. I forget you didn't know him." Franklin had never met his father.

"I think I found my mother's father's peavey at the sale this morning," Franklin said. He had never said more than a few words to his grandfather—his mother wouldn't allow it.

"My husband worked for the paper company and ran the camp where your grandfather worked." Betty nodded. "I've told you that before. Shame what happened to him."

He had never asked her about his grandfather, and she had never volunteered any information. It was possible Franklin's mother had asked her not to say anything to him. Franklin hadn't wanted to upset either his mother or Betty by bringing it up, but finding the peavey at the auction emboldened him.

"Is the story true?" he asked.

She looked over her shoulder out the kitchen window, where her old dog stood in the middle of the field of dead hay, staring into the woods. "I'll tell you what my husband told me when he came back from the woods. The two of them were young then, about your age, maybe younger. They were in camp, I can't remember where, east of the Dead somewhere. Your grandfather and this boy he was partnered with—someone new, Acadian—no, a PEIer—they went out to cut. At the end of the day, your grandfather came back, and the other boy didn't. Your grandfather said the boy had disappeared in the middle of the day. No one said boo about it. No one knows what happened out in the woods between your grandfather and that boy. And that's what I told your mother when she came to ask me about it. It's not like today. There was no time to worry about what happened to the boy and no one pushing to find out. Your grandfather was good at what he did. I once saw him walk a log sideways across the river by spinning it under him. John always said he could have been a master driver, another Don Ross, but I don't doubt he was a hell of a bastard."

Betty rose from her chair and pointed to a jaundiced map on the wall. A blue pen line traced from northern New Hampshire into Maine. She looked at it closely for a moment before stepping away. He had studied this map of the route the logs took to the mill. Small tributaries and brooks had been carefully added and named with a pen. Wiggle Brook was written next to a large X in the top left corner; the course traveled east and south across Little Kennebago Lake, down the Kennebago River, across Cupsuptic and Mooklookmeguntic Lakes, downriver and across the Molly-chunkamunk and Welokennibacook (here the names of Lower and Upper Richardson Lakes were crossed out), over Pond-in-the-River, down Rapid River, across Umbagaog to the Andro-scoggin River, down through Errol Dam, and Pontook Dam, and finally to the mills in Rumford and Lewiston.

When he arrived home, Franklin found a message on the front door of his shop from his friend Mainwaring asking why he had missed lunch. Franklin remembered now that he had been invited to lunch at Mainwaring and Rachel's at 1, but he couldn't remember what he had done after leaving Betty's house. Probably he had just wandered around town; it worried him. He looked at his truck parked on the street, a few inches from the curb. His kitchen was neat; his shop was neat. He touched his stomach. It felt as if he had been sleepwalking, and maybe he had. At nine or ten, he had gone through a stage of sleepwalking all over the house and property. Once his mother found him in the middle of the field, pulling up grass in large fistfuls and tossing it on the ground. Another time he woke in the middle of Vaughn Woods, two miles away, and managed to get back before his mother realized he had left.

In the shop, he reached into his desk for a letter his aunt had written him when his grandfather was found dead. He had read it once a year ago and then never again.

Dear Franklin, this is your aunt Jenny. I know I have not seen you since you were no more than ten I suppose. Your mother and I have not talked much. I heard about the Old Man. I don't know what she, your mother, told you about him. I am hoping not too much. I have not lived with a mean spirit, but I am happy he is gone for good. It has been a long time coming. This way when I am gone and your mother is gone and your uncle Dennis, too, the Old Man will be completely erased from memory. I've felt awfully guilty about you. I'm your godmother, as well as your aunt. In terms of the Old Man, there's no limit to what we cannot know and very little good in it anyway. I am sure you will realize this and leave well enough alone. I am unlikely to ever make it back to Vaughn, but I want you to know that if you ever find your way out to Tucson, you're welcome to stay with me and Bill, whom you have not met. We never had children. In any case, I wanted you to know you are on our minds.

Love, Jenny

Franklin put the letter from his aunt in his pocket and walked up the hill to his mother's house. He didn't know what he would say to her, and when he got there he realized she hadn't come home from work at the hospital. A frayed rope hung from the thickest limb of the white oak and swayed in the breeze. He could see the whole valley from here but could not, no matter how hard he tried, imagine his mother and her sisters as children moving across the yard or his grandfather coming out the front door of what had been, at one time, his house.

In grade school, a kid had told Franklin his grandfather had killed someone years before. Most of the adults in town knew the story but had stopped talking about it because it had happened so long ago. The kid, who had heard the story from his grandfather, told everyone else in class, and though the first version had not included how his grandfather had killed the man, by the time the story wound its way through the whole school back to Franklin, all the details had been added. His grandfather had buried an axe in the back of the man's head. The man had owed his grandfather money; his grandfather had stolen the man's wife; the man had had a gun; his grandfather had had a gun; there had been a duel. Other versions told of how his grandfather had strangled the man with his bare hands. For a brief time, Franklin became a celebrity. Kids looked up from their conversations and watched him walk across the lunchroom. It didn't take long, though, for everyone at school to forget about the story, and Franklin went back to being invisible.

When he asked his mother about the stories, she got up out of her chair and walked out of the room. Franklin's grandmother lived with them then, and her only response was that her ex-husband's family were a bunch of scalp hunters.

"They were not scalp hunters," his mother shouted from the next room. "Don't fill his head with that."

"Massachusetts paid. How do you think they bought this land? I should have realized when I was young—his old man was no good, spent most of his life in the rocker—but because of the war there weren't many boys in my school days," she said. "And my father said he'd mobilize me if I had anything to do with him. That's all it took for me to marry him."

Everyone except Franklin's grandmother called his grandfather the Old Man, when they referred to him at all. Over the years, Franklin had seen his grandfather countless times, driving the opposite direction in his green truck, crossing the street, even down the aisle at Dawson's. Always he pretended not to see Franklin, and Franklin pretended not to see the Old Man.

In his truck, Franklin followed Route 93 through Sweden, then traveled west on 5 and 113 into New Hampshire and north to Route 2, where he turned east until he saw the brown waters of the Androscoggin through the trees. The empty train tracks followed the river, veering away from and then coming back in line with the course of the road. He stopped on several bridges, none of them the iron bridge from the dream he'd had after the flood. North at Bethel, left at Canton, stopping at the boarded-up brick mill in Livermore Falls, where the railroad rejoined, for a short period, the course of the river. No one seemed to live in these towns. After a jog east at Rich's Mountain, he drove almost directly south toward Lewiston while looking into the woods on both sides of the road. Scroungers at auctions told stories of finding skis from horse-drawn sledges, iron fixtures, peavey and pike polls, chains from booms, and other decaying artifacts buried in the new-growth spruce. Most of it worthless. Occasionally people found the site of an old camp and the rusted silhouette of a box or cookstove.

Franklin pictured his grandfather following the boy, a knapsack over one shoulder and his double bitter over the other. Franklin would never know whether his grandfather and the boy had argued or whether his grandfather had come up behind him and simply buried an axe in the back of his head for no reason at all. Maybe the boy hadn't died at all but had simply walked back to Canada.

From a dip in the road where the river veered west into the trees, he thought he saw the outline of a bridge. He pulled off the road and pushed through the brush until he came to a muddy bank. There in the distance stood the iron railroad bridge from his dream the day before. The sky, the tree line, the curve of the bank—everything the same.

He wove through the woods, up a steep rise, and finally stood on the bridge, where he gazed between the iron trusses at the dried-up streambed. Immediately, he wished he hadn't come. He thought of a day in middle school when he had been at Denny Plourde's house down by the river. They weren't close friends, but they hung around each other sometimes. Like him, Denny didn't have many friends. They were sitting in the kitchen of the house when Denny's father came home drunk and announced it was time for their sick dog to be put down. The dog had a lump on its stomach, had stopped eating and started pissing all over the house. Denny's father dragged the dog out of the kitchen, and Denny and Franklin followed. His father tied the dog to a tree and picked up a heavy boulder from the edge of the woods. Denny's father was a big man, and the boulder must have weighed fifty pounds. The dog squirmed out of the way, and the boulder landed on its back and hindquarters. The dog howled so loudly that Franklin crouched and covered his ears. Denny's father picked the boulder up again and this time dropped it on the dog's head. The silence Franklin heard after the dog died was the silence he heard now, standing on the bridge.

Instead of heading to the truck, Franklin followed the tracks into the woods. Snow drifted among the maples. The air didn't even feel cold enough to snow. The path curved. Eventually he came into a field of rotten hay someone had left uncut in the fall. The tracks merged with a mangled road that descended a hill to a group of seven buildings huddled by the river. A church, a manse, a store, and four farmhouses of different shapes. Two identical houses stood next to each other, facing the river. Franklin approached one and looked through the watery glass. Nothing inside, the floors bare. Snow fell more heavily in large tumbling flakes, like the snow in movies. The windows of the store were dark, the cupboards inside bare. Next door, a light burned in the manse and in the upstairs rooms of one other house, but the rest were dark. The sky had darkened, too, covering the fields in shadow.

Following the road in the general direction of his truck, he walked faster as a gust pricked his cheeks. Soon he started to run through the shallow drifts. Sometime in the hours before morning, he drove down Water Street in Vaughn. All the windows of the buildings and houses rising up along the slope of the valley were blue-black in the silver glare of the streetlamps. He parked, and the click of his truck door closing seemed as loud as an explosion. In his shop, shadows stretched along the wall. Over the last few years, the things inside had held his interest when nothing else would—the 150-year-old tables, chairs, lamps, and dressers, the remains of lives that would never come back. He knew the patterns worn into the combs and pipes and canes as well as he knew anyone.

The plow scraped down the middle of the street, sending snow twisting under the lamps, and he imagined he could see all the people who'd ever lived in Vaughn pouring over the cobblestones like fingerlings through a back eddy, come to claim what had once belonged to them. Franklin's grandfather passed among them, the nailed soles of his calked boots snapping along the curb to the time of the shop's mantel clock. Franklin stood and waited for them to enter the store, waited for their demands. As the snow gradually settled, Franklin looked through the window and saw nothing more and nothing less than what was there: the buildings and the curbs and the river that had carved the valley. Nothing remembered, nothing forgotten.

The Wreck of the
Ipswich Sparrow
(2000)

Phoebe Hutchinson Howland

In April 2000, the white clapboard house on the corner of Second Street and Litchfield Road in Vaughn came on the market for the first time since its construction in 1770. The house appeared grand and square, but by stating that the new owners would need to update an otherwise fine example of Georgian style retaining many original features, the Century 21 website was acknowledging that it was held together by horsehair and lead paint. Though the roof might last another winter, and the knob-and-tube wiring appeared intact, the battleship of an oil furnace might explode at any moment, a dark shellac of bacon grease sealed the rusty metal cabinets and drop ceiling of the 1951 kitchen, the sills absorbed and shed water like a sink sponge, the chimney and walls housed a colony of red squirrels, and many of the south-facing windows were held in place by the strength of the glass. The Realtor, Mary Simpson, was counting on out-of-state buyers with spare cash and romantic notions about the past.

The day after the listing went live the father of the current owners called Mary Simpson from his home in San Mateo, California, announced his name, John Carlton Howland, and complained that Mary had no right to "give away" the oldest structure in town (a claim that she disproved in thirty seconds of online research), which had been built by one of his ancestors.

"But it doesn't belong to you *specifically* anymore, am I right?" she asked as politely as possible, and he hung up on her, which seemed an okay result. She recognized his name and assumed that he was related to old John Howland, who still lived in town.

The next day one of the two current owners—the son of the man she had talked to the day before—called from Oregon to complain that the asking price was "absurdly low." He claimed that Benedict Arnold had stayed in the house for three nights during his failed 1775 expedition up the Kennebec River to take Quebec from the English—an expedition, he pointed out, that had included members of his own family. Mary replied that the Benedict Arnold thing raised interesting possibilities (though from a real estate perspective, not so much) and asked if he had any corroborating evidence. The great weapon of the Realtor: ask the owner to check on that. He agreed to check, but he felt sure that they should be asking twice as much for the house, and he didn't feel confident that his sister and the Realtor really knew what they were doing.

"What would make you feel more confident?" she asked in the same neutral tone she used for anyone who called from south of Freeport.

"More money," he said.

The other owner—the son's sister, Phoebe—the main person Mary Simpson had been communicating with, thank God—

also called to say that she would arrive soon from California to empty the house. Phoebe seemed to have a reasonable sense of the house's value, which was apparently not very much by West Coast standards.

Mary told Phoebe that someone might buy the house in order to tear it down because the land, which was located just a block from Water Street, had more value than the house. Phoebe mentioned historic zoning, and Mary said, "You haven't lived here in a while, dear. We have no such thing."

When her father decided to deed the house in Vaughn to Phoebe and her brother the year before, he had just survived a heart attack and had given up eating meat and cheese. He transferred the house in a hurry, Phoebe assumed, because he thought he might die of the same heart troubles that had killed his mother. After they cleaned out his pipes (as he described it) in Palo Alto, he went home with an approved menu of vegetables. Skinny but angry, he began power walking through the neighborhood twice a day and seemed ten years younger.

When she realized that her father wouldn't die soon, Phoebe offered to give the house back (though she doubted that her brother would agree), but he waved her off. "Are you sure?" she said. "Once you give it away, it's not yours anymore." As a lawyer, she had experience with people not thinking things through, and she knew that her father desperately wanted to return to Vaughn and the house where he'd grown up. He didn't want to die in California, which she understood. In Vaughn, you ended up in the family plot with a giant stone; in San Mateo, she didn't know what happened. You ended up in a ceramic urn on a shelf. But her father couldn't retire yet. Her parents didn't have enough money to retire, and the house in San Mateo still had a huge mortgage, and the house in Maine needed work her father once would have undertaken on his own. It would cost a fortune to pay someone else to do it.

"What's done is done," he said, but Phoebe felt confident that he hadn't fathomed the implications of this statement.

Phoebe's brother, who lived with his barely legal girlfriend in Portland, Oregon, where he worked in a bakery, had no children, and smoked pot daily with his employers, wanted the money from the house so that he could start a vintage bicycle restoration business. Phoebe, who worked a million hours a week for a law firm in Palo Alto, had two kids, and had recently separated from her husband—if that's what you call it when one party decides to stop dealing with reality—needed the money so she wouldn't lose her overpriced Cracker Jacks shack in Palo Alto.

"It has to be done," her brother said in the congested tone he had acquired in the Northwest and asked if she would mind flying to Vaughn to take care of the sale. She knew how to handle these kinds of things. By *things* he meant life, and he was right.

When Phoebe dropped her kids off at her parents' house on the way to the airport, they ran inside to their room, arranged with more books and toys than they had at home, and didn't even say goodbye. Their grandmother, who had worked for years as a surly disciplinarian in an elementary school classroom in Maine, had turned into an enabler of constant fun: video games, Ben and Jerry's, staying up until nine. It wasn't the childhood Phoebe remembered, when ice cream appeared as regularly as fireworks.

As Phoebe headed for her car, her mother asked her to remember to bring back Aunt Helen's trunk. "Your father doesn't want it to end up in some pawnshop."

"Aunt Helen? The old ratty trunk in the guest room?"

"You know what I'm talking about," her mother scolded.

"Why doesn't Dad come out and ask me himself?" Phoebe could hear her father on the back patio, listening to some game on his transistor radio. Even though he had refused to take it back, he couldn't forgive her for selling the house. Her brother didn't merit blame. In the meantime, she now had to worry about this long-dead aunt, who was not actually an aunt, if Phoebe remembered correctly, but an ancestor of some sort—one of many to have lived in that old house. The room to the right at the top of the stairs had always been called "Aunt Helen's room"—except by Phoebe's mother, who, in rebellion against a house whose every nook signified a history not her own, had always refused to call it anything but "the guest room."

Fine, Phoebe told her mother to tell her father that she would bring back the trunk of this person.

The house had once belonged to Aunt Helen, who inherited it from her father and deeded it late in life to her nephew, Phoebe's great-uncle, who deeded it to Phoebe's father. Otherwise, the house never would have passed down to Phoebe and her brother. Phoebe discovered the record in the copy of the deed she took to read on the plane. She also found an old will that detailed how Aunt Helen had not been the intended beneficiary. Aunt Helen's brother and only sibling had died before their father, leaving Aunt Helen as the sole heir. In deeding the house to her nephew, Aunt Helen may have wanted help caring for the old house. According to Phoebe's mother, Aunt Helen had no children of her own. Phoebe's father had never said much about Aunt Helen.

When Phoebe parked the rental car in front of the house in Vaughn, she could see that the house had "fallen into habits indicative of self-loathing," as her former Palo Alto therapist would've said. She walked around the outside, pressing her hands into clapboards, face boards, and windowsills. In several places her finger passed through the carapace of paint and sank up to her knuckle in wood softened to moss. She pulled a rusted iron nail out of a clapboard and snapped it in half as if it were a toothpick. In the bathroom, the floor at the foot of the tub compressed like a spring. A pile of mortar and broken bricks had collected in the hearth.

The air warmed in the afternoon, and it was hot for midsummer in Maine or even California. Phoebe hadn't slept much in the last weeks, and instead of organizing the contents of the house, she threw open the window sashes in the parlor, lay down on the cool pine floor in her shorts and T-shirt, and pressed her skin against the wood. Before long a thunderhead darkened the sky, gusts sent the pale leaves of the maple in the yard into a boil, and rain splotched the window glass. The air charged with electricity as the temperature dropped, and a flash made her start counting as she had as a child: "one-one thousand, two-one thousand . . ." The next flash brought the deluge. After ten minutes, the sky slowly cleared, steam rose off the asphalt, and cars sizzled past on Second Street.

Later in the afternoon she walked from room to room over the shifting and groaning planks and tried to decide what of the paintings, dark tables, chairs and bureaus she should ship back to her parents. The closets were full of dishes, wooden bowls, silver piled with old boots, canvas coats, and small folding wallets containing daguerreotypes and tintypes of relatives she had never known and couldn't identify. Trunks were crammed with piles of old deeds, letters, and documents written in the scrawl of the time. And there was more in the attic: blanket chests filled with moth-eaten woollens, two old flags the length of coffins, books both on shelves and stacked on the floor in wooden crates, all of it covered in dust. Coughing so badly she thought she would crack a rib, she began to separate everything into two piles: one for storage, one to give away. If she asked her father what she should save, he would say, "All of it." He was reliably unhelpful.

In the small south-facing room at the top of the stairs—"Aunt Helen's room"—sat the old pale-blue sea trunk with the name "Capt. J. M. Howland" stenciled on the lid, a simple pine bureau with an old hurricane lamp, a pine rope bed, and a worn hooked rug on the floor. The wide pine floors in the rest of the house were unpainted, but the planks in this room had always been a light gray.

In the top drawer of the bureau someone had left several articles from the *Kennebec Journal* about Aunt Helen's life when she turned 105 in 1934. The newsprint was faded and torn to the point where Phoebe had to hold the articles under the light from the window. She read the caption under a photo showing Aunt Helen sitting in a rocking chair with some sort of giant bird in her lap.

Kennebec Journal, August 7, 1934

A Life Full of Courage, Independence, and Often Joy

Miss Helen Jacobs Howland, life-long resident of Vaughn and one of the oldest living people in the United States, turns 105 today. Her age and vitality stupefy many. Born in Vaughn in 1829, she grew up traveling around the world with her family. Her father, Captain John Mainwaring Howland, was one of the town's prominent sea captains and made many trips to India and China. After she finished traveling the world with her parents, Miss Helen Jacobs returned to Vaughn and lived the rest of her days in the home where she was born and had grown up. She never married and has been very active in town life all these years. A graduate of the teacher's college at the University of Maine in Farmington, she worked in the library until she was 93 and volunteered in the local school until just a few years ago.

As she grew older, she needed some assistance with household chores but was otherwise active both in and outside of her home. Driving her nephew's Buick was one of her favorite activities; Miss Helen Jacobs decided to quit driving when she turned 103—a decision that was entirely her own.

"It was not because I was pulled over by the police or had an accident," she insisted during the interview in the Second Street home where she lives with her nephew, John Hayes Howland, and his family. "I just stopped driving." At 105, she still doesn't need a hearing aid, and her eyeglasses sit unused on a table-board most of the time. She and her nephew showed us her room and her enormous 20-year-old parrot, whose name is Polly. The massive bird swooped around the room, sat at her feet, and called Miss Helen Jacobs by name several times during the interview.

"She is really a unique person; she is wired differently than the rest of us," John Howland, her nephew, said. "She takes life as it comes and doesn't worry about things." She loves to play cards, especially bridge, spades, and cribbage. She also keeps busy with crossword and jigsaw puzzles. She can often be found having a cup of tea while looking out the window at the river from her rocking chair. She particularly loves when the Maine lupine flowers are in bloom, and her favorite flowers are orchids. When someone complains that economic times are tough, she says: "This is nothing."

And how does she stay so healthy?

"I mind my own business," she said. "I've outlived a lot of them," she added, "but it's just another birthday, and goodness knows I've had enough of them."

When we saw that she had a radio on her bureau, we asked her about the new music, and she said, "They sing but they can't sing. They holler. So that's no good."

Helen Jacobs is somewhat frail but independent and courageous in spirit, and her mind maintains an iron grip on memories and dates. She doesn't hesitate when asked if she still enjoys life.

"Most things are in the past," she said. "I have a good appetite, and I love dessert."

Phoebe had to be back at work in less than a week—she shouldn't have been paying any attention to the trunk—but she picked up Aunt Helen's journal for a quick look. For several years after Aunt Helen started the journal she wrote very little and simply pasted in clippings from the *Kennebec Gazette*, which later became the *Kennebec Journal*, of "Arrivals" and "Sailings," as well as reports of "Wrecks" and "Piracies." *Schr Rob Roy, Capt C. Bassett, of this town, for Portland, capsized in a white squall, Thursday afternoon off Boon Island; had carried no ballast. Schr Charlotte Ann was boarded by a gang of desperados in the harbor of Havana for the purpose of plundering. They had long knives. A fight ensued and the Charlotte Ann and her crew all lost.* When she did write, she spoke of wanting to go to sea with her father. "When I turn 14, so he says," she wrote three months before her fourteenth birthday. But when she finally turned fourteen, she wrote, "He says not now. I think he wants me here forever. Here I only read about what happens, and we know nothing of life." At the bottom of the page, she drew a sketch of a ship in Calcutta Harbor that she may have copied from another drawing—possibly from one of the many sketches in her father's logs.

Aunt Helen must have felt as if her real life—the one she longed to live—waited for her beyond the mouth of the river. Phoebe had trouble imagining a time when Vaughn felt at all connected to the rest of the world. In her time, strangers never showed up unless they passed through on their way to Augusta or headed farther north to the Allagash or maybe Katahdin. People from far away did not bring news of the world, and people from town did not regularly set out for anyplace farther away than Portland.

When Phoebe turned fourteen, her last year before high school, she started spending a lot of time lying on the floor, often in Aunt Helen's room, staring at the ceiling, not thinking of Bombay or Calcutta or Havana, not thinking at all, really. Now she lay on the horsehair mattress in Aunt Helen's room and in the pages of one of the calfskin journals found drawings of houses and boats in crayon that she would not have recognized as her own if she had not signed her name, PHOEBE, in a large purple scrawl. When the light failed, she read by the light of a small flashlight she kept in her purse. Despite the open window, the air in the room didn't move. Several times she went to the window to watch the moonlit current of the Kennebec push south toward the open ocean.

Phoebe's father had never met Aunt Helen. One time he said offhandedly that the old woman talked to herself in her own room, a detail he probably heard from his uncle, who had also grown up in this house and who lived with his wife in the ell until he died. Phoebe's great-uncle had once mentioned that he'd been afraid as a child to walk by Aunt Helen's door. Either she gave him nickels wrapped in scraps of paper or she handed him obituaries cut from the *Kennebec Journal*, trying to impress on him, before he even understood that people were born, how frequently they seemed to die.

Phoebe didn't understand how a girl who'd never left Maine and had barely traveled outside her hometown could help but feel paralyzed by the idea of setting out with a captain who had to rely on inaccurate charts and a brass compass and sextant. Of course, Helen would not have dwelled on the instruments because she knew her father always returned from the sea and never, she wrote, suffered from bad luck or human error. Maybe the possibility of drowning felt insignificant compared to the fear of spending her whole life in her bedroom.

Phoebe had feared the same thing at fourteen. The spring before they moved to California she applied for a job at the new Dairy Queen on the road to Augusta so she would have enough money her second year of high school to buy her own car and drive herself and her friends Kim and Stacey out to the Monmouth lakes, where Kim's parents had a cabin. Some girls she knew already had boyfriends with cars, but Kim and Stacey both agreed not to acquire boyfriends. A Chevette, nothing fancy; she could swing it on savings from months of serving ice cream at the Queen, would take them out Vaughn Road to Outlet Road to Farm Road to Collins Road to Pond Road, where they would drive north with the windows down and look over their shoulders to the big lake and think, *that's* not where we're going—not the lake where people roared around in loud, stupid boats. They would head to the smaller Carlton Pond, where the cool water lapped the shore in the August heat. Kim's parents would let them use the cabin by themselves. Not overnight, but still. They would float on the raft under the sun while the fish swam beneath them. In Phoebe's mind, and in the minds of her friends, the next year had already arrived and they were already on the raft with the Chevette parked next to the cabin.

Before she had a chance to scoop her first cone, however, Phoebe's mother came into her room and announced that the family would move to Portsmouth before the fall. When the governor had changed, Phoebe's father had lost his job in Augusta, and he had been out of work for more than half a year now. "Your father and I don't want to go, but this is a really good opportunity. There are not a lot of jobs anywhere right now. If things go well, who knows, maybe we can come back before too long." Her mother's arms hung at her sides like a pair of tools the world no longer needed.

Phoebe knew nothing about Portsmouth, even though it was only two and a half hours away; she dug in and said she wouldn't go. She had all her friends—girls she'd known her whole life—and planned (hoped) to play softball for the University of Maine, where most of her friends would go after high school. She thought she might live in Portland for a few years after college, just to try out a city, but then she would move back to Vaughn. If they moved to Portsmouth, none of it—nothing—would happen.

Her mother did not seem sympathetic. She only said, "You'll adjust. You'll make new friends." To Phoebe, who had lived nowhere else but here and known only these people, her mother's words may as well have been spoken in French.

When Phoebe's flashlight flickered and dimmed, she turned it off and sat in darkness. Mice pattered in the attic above and skittered down the inside of the walls. In her bare feet, she felt her way along the planks of the hall and down the stairs. Moonlight shone on the kitchen table, where her father had read the paper every morning before work. The chairs sat at different angles to the table. She found matches in the drawer, lit the hurricane lamp that sat on a shelf, and climbed the stairs. The light illuminated the plaster walls. In the upstairs hallway, she froze. The door to Aunt Helen's room was open at the end of the hall. Of course it was— she had left it open—but she had a sense now that Aunt Helen waited for her in the room, sitting in her chair with the enormous parrot standing on her knee. By the time she reached the end of the hallway, she could see the chair, empty in the corner, and the journal, open where she had left it on the bed.

In the end Helen did not go to sea with her family. Over the next three years, she filled her journal sporadically with reports of what others had seen and done in other places, and then for months at a time she wrote very little or nothing at all.

In 1848, following her marriage to Captain Robert William Pingree of Machias, Helen finally went to sea. With only a few words about her husband (tall, mustached, a skilled captain), she filled her journal with descriptions of the birds that followed them off shore, the porpoises and whales, the crew of the brig *Ipswich Sparrow* ("a poor miserable set"), and the storm as they rounded the Cape of Good Hope ("The wind blew hard and the sea rolled mountains high and we did not know if our house on deck would go to pieces, but it stood yet. The galley went over one night breaking the stove and everything that was in it: two iron boilers, one large pot. It continued to rage with increased fury, every wave seemed as if it would swallow us up and roared so dreadfully that the sound is still running in my ears. About eight a.m. Mr. Cheever on a mission to Calcutta read the 107 Psalm, the truths of which we felt then if never before").

Helen's billowing cursive slanted to the right like sails bent under the wind. In June, they anchored off Point Balasore and waited for a pilot to take them to Calcutta. At Kedgeree, the first village heading upriver, they rode ashore in boats made of sewn bark and rowed by men naked except for a bit of cloth below the waist. In Calcutta, the wide streets filled with men. "Our house is brick and we live on the second floor," she wrote. "Robert's banian also lives in such a house and his palanquin bearers rest outside when he is inside. We go to the Red Church, the English church. Services are at nine on Sunday. In the evening we walk on the Esplanade that leads up to the Fort. On the way back to the house one afternoon, I saw a man whose hand was the size of the cushion of a chair. He kept uttering 'buckshish' to Robert and me. Captain Dole told us to ignore him. Robert threw a rupee at him anyway, and the man followed us, saying 'buckshish' in my ear and waving his giant hand in the heat. Robert said that half the people in the world were born with saddles on their backs and the other half born to ride those people to death. I asked him how he thought of such a thing and he replied he did not. It was a saying from Montesquieu."

Several months after she arrived in Calcutta, Helen wrote, "I am pregnant. More than five months now."

Robert told Helen that she must stay at home and not wander out—especially not alone. If she had to go out while he worked, his banian or one of their friends from Maine or Newburyport could accompany her. She did not listen, though—she "could not," she wrote. She couldn't sleep when Robert left to sail up the coast to Bombay, Colombo, Madras, and ports on the Malabar Coast. She thought of people in their circle of friends she might visit— William Pingree, Mary Dole, Alice Wingate, Lucinda Crosby— but it seemed to her as if she did not know these people except "by circumstance." They were all from Maine and lived together here in this place where she had come with her husband—because of her husband.

At home she sat by an open window on the second floor. She never lit the lamps at night but lay down when the light failed. One morning she told the house staff they could leave. They didn't understand at first and just stood looking at the floor. She had Robert's banian translate that she wanted them to leave. Helen gave them much of the money Robert had left her to use and asked them not to come back. "I dismissed them, but for no fault of their own," Phoebe read.

Several days later she left through the back entrance so that the servants might not see, though of course there were no servants. As Helen described walking through the heat, Phoebe felt the strain in her thighs and the burn on the skin of her neck. When it grew too hot, she rested in the shade. Late in the afternoon, she walked again, lost now as she turned down one street after another until she found the river. A quarter mile up the bank a crowd of people gathered. When she drew closer, she saw that they surrounded a man's body wrapped in cloth on a pile of sticks: "The poor widow sat on a cot frame next to her husband's corpse with her two small sons about her and a large crowd of women and men both. They pulled brush on top of the sticks until the pile was four feet tall, and they wet flax in the river. The poor wife got upon her feet with a small basket in hand. The four men took the dead corpse of her husband and laid it on the pile of sticks with his head to the northward. The wife was assisted by the men to step off the cot frame. I thought she was going to step away. A man rubbed red paint in her hair, and she walked round the pile three times in which her husband lay and laid herself down alongside of her husband with her right hand under his neck. All those around immediately hove on brush and wood. There were four men with green bamboos, and I didn't understand at first why, and then I understood. To hold her down in case she should not be able to stand the flames. After they had piled on brush enough, they poured on some oil and flour of brimstone. All this done, her two sons came round the pile with lighted torches. The eldest of them set fire to the pile toward her head and the other toward her feet. The natives made such a noise that I could not hear the last groan, but I saw when the pile was all in flames that she turned over on her back."

After the funeral ceremony, Helen felt sick and walked to Lucinda Crosby's home. The English doctor came and stood beside the bed next to a Hindoo in full dress who bowed deeply. Servants with flowing pants and turbans of the purest white lined the wall. Mary Dole looked down at her. Lucinda told Helen that she had a fever and that she should lie down. As soon as her head rested on a cushion, she fell asleep. She later learned that the doctor had been afraid she would lose the baby, but she did not. She stayed with the Crosbys for several weeks, until Robert arrived. She told him the story of what had happened and apologized. She had been foolish. She had not done as he had asked her to do. He said that everything would be all right now. The doctor had explained that women could become confused on their own, especially during pregnancy. Robert never should have left her.

Several months later she gave birth to William Howland Pingree, and from that time on it was as if a light had been turned out and Helen disappeared from her journals. Phoebe found only brief reports about Robert's business interests and the baby. Like the shipping reports in the *Kennebec Gazette*, only the barest details remained.

Phoebe and her family did not move to Portsmouth after all. The job opportunity fell through at the same time that another opened up in California. So, with only a month's warning, they packed up their car and drove across the country. Phoebe knew about California from TV, of course. The Brady Bunch lived there, and the Partridge Family, but those weren't real people.

When Phoebe first woke in her new bedroom in California two months after she had turned fifteen, she saw that her mother had arranged the bookcase, the bed, and the bureau exactly as they had been set up in Vaughn. One morning her father returned from the wilderness of stoplights and shopping centers with a box of donuts and called for everyone to load into the station wagon. They were going to see the Pacific. Phoebe told her mother that she didn't want to go, but she didn't dare say anything to her father, whose enthusiasm seemed as fragile as a teacup.

Her father pulled off the road on the way to the coast and marched to an enormous tree. "Come here," he said with his hand pressed against the bark. She did as he told her to and fit her fingers into the grooves of the "skin," as her father called it, of one of the oldest living things on earth. "Look up," he said. Light filtered through the canopy. She would not have been surprised to see a dinosaur run through the woods.

They drove out of the hills, parked in a lot off Route 1, and followed their father along a wooden boardwalk and stairs to a wide beach that seemed to extend endlessly in both directions. Down the beach a man threw a tennis ball into the foaming wash for his dog, which rushed into the water again and again. When the man strolled farther away, he and his dog vanished in a wave of dissolving light.

Weeks passed, and months; her father went to work in the mornings, her mother started a garden, her brother came home with new friends, and no one at her new high school even noticed that she was new. One among three hundred sophomores, many of them new to the area like her, she blended in as long as she didn't speak. Her accent gave her away.

Her father soon left his big job opportunity, which had not turned out as well as he had hoped. The politics of the people he worked for failed to meet his standards, meaning he had alienated them right away. Within a week, he found another job that did not pay as well and was not what anyone would call an opportunity, he claimed. A person needed a job, he told the family over supper, and none existed in Maine—not for him. Phoebe recognized her father's familiar journey from prideful rebellion to self-pity. He seemed to know nothing in between. In an effort to not be like him (her mother had often said Phoebe and her father were just alike), Phoebe decided to stop sulking. She stopped writing to her friends in Vaughn. It seemed to her then, as it did now, that a person could not live in more than one place at a time.

Less than a year ago a man at Phoebe's law firm named Ernst had put his hand on her elbow, which he had done before, though not exactly in this way. Born in Munich, Ernst was one of those childless lawyers who'd never marry a second time. He was discreet and skittish, but disciplined. A little slouchy in his linen suits, he always kept his head down. When he turned to her and asked if she would meet him after work, she didn't hesitate. They went to a bar where they had gone with their colleagues many times. After one drink, they took his car to his condo, just four blocks away.

She'd been afraid when she was young that she could vanish into a man's life, but it turned out that this had never been a danger. After she and Ernst had sex, she stepped onto his redwood balcony in her underwear and stood in the dark. Her husband and kids would not think her absence strange, as she often worked late. Dressed in slippers and nothing else, Ernst joined her on the deck with two glasses of wine. He kept his place simple, modern, with generic leather furniture: one bookcase, one picture of two old people, probably his parents, and one of a man a bit younger than Ernst, probably his brother. Everything he cared about would fit in two boxes.

"I still think I will move back to Germany someday," he said, "but probably I won't." He smiled briefly, his lips stretching across his closed mouth. In the moonlight his skin looked like milk, and for a moment she imagined what he must have looked like as a boy, before law school.

When she first met her husband, Michael, in college, he dreamed of becoming a pilot and covered his dorm wall with posters of airplanes. He was also a Marxist and an English major. She felt then as if they were embarking on a great journey together. Now she couldn't remember what it felt like to be with him; she couldn't remember the details of their wedding.

The whole thing—stocks, companies, jobs, real estate—collapsed for everyone they knew, and their house, suddenly worth nearly half as much as they owed on it, felt like a prison. Since his start-up had gone under the previous year, Michael had trouble getting out of bed in the morning. Even though he stayed at home all day, he forgot to pick the kids up at school, to pick up items at the grocery store, to pay the bills. He went to a doctor and took medication but soon stopped, claiming he wasn't depressed—that wasn't his trouble. At supper he blinked like a giant owl at the kids. He asked them about their days as if reading from a script.

He refused to look at her. After the kids went to sleep, he spoke (when he spoke at all) of the unfairness of the system. The people who always won would always win, and everyone else could fight over the scraps.

It seemed to her now that even in college he had become discouraged easily. After they married, he took up long-distance running. Leaving the house early in the morning and after work, he spent hours on the back roads that wound into the hills. Phoebe's father said that she browbeat him. She could no more say when Michael had begun to vanish than she could say if he'd ever been fully with them in the first place. Hindsight was no gift and no more accurate than predicting the future.

In the last months he'd begun retreating to the room they used as a study. At night she heard him lie down on the blow-up camping mattress spread out next to the desk. Sometimes she stood outside the door and listened for the sound of his breathing, the tapping of his fingers on the computer, or the turning of pages. Nothing. One night she couldn't take it anymore and pushed open the door. He lay on his mattress reading *A Short History of England*. She told him that businesses collapse, marriages falter—a speech she had prepared in her head. She wanted to confess about Ernst but didn't. He lowered the book and shielded the cover with his hand. "What?" he said.

Phoebe leaned back in Helen's chair and looked at the lamplight pooling on the ceiling. According to her phone, it was 2 a.m.—too late to call anyone in either time zone. What she needed to do was sell the house in Vaughn and return to California. She'd already wasted most of her first day (and now the night) holed up next to the trunk.

The newspaper story and obituary about Helen had wrongly stated that she had never married. Helen not only had married, but had a child. In the bottom of the trunk she found a cheap cardboard notebook, which Helen must have purchased later in life.

Phoebe remembered seeing the notebook when she was young, but the flimsy, dull cover had not tempted her. Opening it now, she found no children's drawings—no sign that anyone had ever read what Helen had written on the blue pages.

A newspaper clipping from the *Kennebec Gazette* pasted on the inside cover of the notebook stated, "Wrecked—the Brig Ipswich Sparrow on the outer bar east of Sable Island during gale February 10, 1854, Capt. Robert Pingree, family and crew all lost."

But no—not all lost. The wife, the mother, Helen—Aunt Helen—lived another eighty-one years.

The scratchy handwriting below the clipping in the notebook contrasted with the long, loopy letters in the earlier journals written more than half a century before, but Phoebe sensed Helen in the writing. The notebook was signed "Helen Pingree" below the newspaper clipping.

Phoebe carried the lamp down the hall to the landing, where the floor-to-ceiling bookcase contained random books and encyclopaedias that her parents had left behind. The entry on Sable Island described a treeless crescent of sand a hundred miles east of Nova Scotia. Nothing more than a beach held together by grass, the island contained neither rock nor pebble, and when Phoebe looked at a map in the atlas she couldn't understand at first why Helen and Robert had found themselves there. The article explained that ships heading to and from Europe commonly blundered within a mile of the island's south bar. In Helen's day, a wreck on Sable would have surprised no one. More than 350 ships and 10,000 lives had been lost on the long bars that extended in some cases 18 miles out from the shore of an island 26 miles long and 1 mile wide and never rising higher than a hundred feet above sea level. Waves just offshore reached a height of a hundred feet, and winds had been clocked at 174 miles per hour. Some of the ships wrecked there vanished within minutes, smashed to pieces by the surf and swallowed by the sand.

"In the middle of the night we heard a grinding and crushing noise, such as one might suppose would arise from striking on rocks," Phoebe read in Helen's notebook. "It was caused by the breaking of the rudder chain, Robert said. Though our ship had struck the sandbar bow on, it slowly swung round till her stern also struck. Surf crashed over the bulwarks and flowed into the cabin. We could not see the island—only the white flash of the crashing surf. Robert ordered the crew to tie casks of fish oil to the deck, tie one man to each cask, and tie a ladle to each man. Then the men started to ladle out the oil. The waves rose to the height of the mast but smoothed out around the ship and ceased breaking over the deck when the oil did its work. Robert spotted the lifeboat when it was almost on us and told me to go with William and our passengers, the Hiltons and the Hills. One moment the lifeboat was far below, and the next it was in height halfway up the mast. We were meant to climb in at the right moment, but when that time came William broke free and ran back to the cabin for his books. Robert picked me up bodily and lifted me down against my will to one of the men in the lifeboat. The man rowing assured me my husband and son would be on the next boat.

"The sun began to rise, and I saw how it was with us. The surf rolled in three rows of breakers, now in a hurried rush and again more slowly; here would appear a break, a calm area, but the next moment the same spot was the most dangerous I had ever seen. The men already on shore were making signs where to land. Twice we backed water and waited.

"'Here we go, then, in the name of God,' the steersman said. He told us to put on life preservers, but there were not enough so I had to go without. A wave washed over us, and in a moment we were carried on over the top of a crest and found our boat on shore. Men rushed into the water to carry us to land and draw up the boat. We sat down on a little hillock of sand. Birds began flying wildly about our heads. We soon saw the reason: the ground around us was filled with nests. We could hardly stretch out our hands without touching either their eggs or the young birds, little downy things.

"We watched the lifeboat leave for another load, and after some delay it started from the ship. The surf was worse, and the boat overloaded, so that only two oars were in use. They came slowly hesitating, then tossing about helplessly. We saw the boat with its cargo, one moment on top of a tall wave, the next moment vanished from sight in a trough. In addition to Robert and William, there were several passengers and the crew who had not come in the first trip. Some of our party on the beach ran about, others knelt in prayer. Next we saw the lifeboat start to bottom upwards. To my surprise it righted itself. I remember seeing sharply outlined against the sky the figure of a man with an oar in his hand, standing in the boat trying to guide its course. While we gazed, the boat rose up and hurled end over end.

"Two dead bodies washed up with white foam on their lips. They were two of the passengers, but not Robert and William. The superintendent of the Humane Establishment said that the ladies would go to his house and the rest of the sailors to the sailors' building, but those of us on shore would not move until everyone from the upset lifeboat could be found. Sarah Hilton walked the beach, asking everyone over and over if they had seen her husband. With the wind rising and the temperature dropping, the superintendent and his men forced us to move inland. Robert and William were still missing.

"Our meal consisted of bread, beef, potatoes and sea biscuits, but few could eat. When night came on, the cries of those who had lost people in the lifeboat were truly heart-rending. I walked slowly from the superintendent's house to where the horses were kept and there, by the roaring of the sea and the whistling of the winds, was sheltered from their doleful cries until I grew too cold and had to return. The superintendent's wife told me that when the sand got bad in my eyes I should open the door of the kitchen stove and let the smoke cause tears to wash the sand away."

The next morning, one of the life-saving crew brought her trunk, which had washed ashore. On opening the lid, she did not recognize the swollen mass—the feathers of a dead bird, maybe, all lying wet—but her journals wrapped in oilcloth remained dry. A ship's bell rang, and the superintendent's wife said that all should meet in the barn for a prayer service by the superintendent.

Helen wandered away from the small compound of buildings and over a dune onto a hillock. A wild stallion appeared and approached with a fierce trot, passing Helen to the right before disappearing. Helen might have thought that the wild Sable ponies that Phoebe read about in the encyclopaedia, marooned on the island since 1738 and roaming the dunes in packs, were the largest horses she'd ever seen. According to the entry, with no trees on the island people lost all sense of scale. Helen later saw four more stallions that at first sight ran and halted on a sand cliff. Their manes stretched down to their hooves and plumes of steam poured from their nostrils and mouths. Maybe because of their bared teeth, they seemed to laugh at her. One of the bolder ponies ran toward her with such a "direful appearance" that Helen thought she would be trampled. The stallion stopped no more than five feet in front of her, snorted, and flared its nostrils. As suddenly as they had arrived, they vanished, leaving her alone again.

On top of the next sand cliff, Helen saw the beach where she had landed in the lifeboat and the bar where the *Ipswich Sparrow* had grounded. The waves continued to rise high and break as they reached the shallows. Seeing no sign of her husband's ship either in the waves or on the beach, she sat down on the dune to wait for her family. Soon an object appeared dead to windward. At first she mistook it for a large bird, but then she saw a sail five or six miles distant running before a dark mass of clouds. No vessel could survive such mountains of water. She thought to warn the superintendent, but then she saw the life-saving crew arrive on the beach.

When the ship approached within three miles of land, waves on each side curled as high as the tips of the masts and fell with the weight of hundreds of tons. Waves breaking close to the island created troughs so deep that they touched sand. Breaking from the bottom, they appeared angry as they fell. The ship hit, and the force of the waves smashed her to pieces within minutes. Helen waited for the superintendent and his men to launch their boats, but they stood on shore. Maybe with the ship so far out, and the seas too rough, nothing could be done. Within moments, it seemed to Helen, nothing remained where there had been a ship. The life-saving crew shovelled sand into the bottoms of the twenty-five-foot lifeboats, but the wind still dragged the hulls along the beach.

Despite the cold, she began each day by hiking over the dunes to the beach and waited there, as she put it, "for any sign of them." Helen must have meant their bodies, Phoebe thought, though she might have hoped Robert and William would walk out of the surf unharmed. If such a thing could happen anywhere, it could happen here. One evening the superintendent's wife described a ship that had been swallowed in one hour and then unearthed five years later during another storm. The bones of the crew still wore their clothes, and the cargo of Irish linens looked as clean as the day the ship had set sail.

For two days Helen could not go to the beach because of another storm, and on the third day she found scattered human bones—not on the beach but high in the dunes. She couldn't decide at first how the bones had ended up four hundred yards or more from the tide line. The place where she now stood must have once been at the edge of the sea or possibly underwater. The island itself moved with the shifting currents and storms. The dunes changed shape in the wind. When they reached a certain height, the wind blew holes in their walls and carried sand out to sea. The length of the island grew every summer and shrank by a mile every winter, the superintendent's wife said. The long underwater sandbars contracted and swelled, Phoebe imagined, like an underwater lung. Though water deepened the farther one moved from the island, the superintendent's wife told the story one evening of how the crew of a schooner anchored in thirty-five fathoms of water out of sight of land discovered that a sandbar had approached like a whale and surfaced off their stern.

Another storm hit the following week, keeping her at the superintendent's compound. When she finally returned to the spot where she had found the bones, only windswept sand remained. Offshore a pod of porpoises tumbled head-over-heels. At this point, Helen lost track of her memories of what happened in the sand. She lost herself in the days, in the light and dark, in the pounding of the surf shaking her spine, in the blowing wind and sand, and in the arrival of more storms, which seemed, like the waves they produced, to arrive in groups of three. Just as one wave could have three foaming heads, what she first took for three storms might have been one storm with three layers of ferocity. She sensed—no, she *knew* that Robert and William were some-where on the island. She could not imagine leaving.

She ate meals in the superintendent's house, sitting next to the superintendent's wife, but she began to sleep in the horse barn and wander during the day. The waves and hills of sand shifted amidst the grass. Past the shallow lake at the center of the island, she found the roof of a house half buried in a dune. At first she thought the roof must have blown free from one of the compound buildings and sailed across the island, but then she discovered a chimney. Next to the chimney a hole in the shingles opened to an upstairs bedroom. The roof had not blown off the house; the sand had surrounded the building. Elsewhere under her feet lay buried the rest of the first station the superintendent's wife had described. The sand had risen so quickly over a period of days that they hadn't been able to break down the buildings for lumber. They had to leave for the other side of the island before the island swallowed them.

She crawled through the opening, and Phoebe pictured her following the wall with the edges of her fingers, stepping care-fully from room to room until she saw the chimney and the hole in the roof through which the sun shone. She lay down on the gray boards, and Phoebe saw a shaft of light arc like the hand of a clock across her shoulders and arm and climb the wall until it disappeared, sinking the room in darkness. At some point the moon appeared in the hole above, and silver light collected at her fingertips. In the morning a light as warm as lamplight poured through the hole and with it a stream of pale green sand that collected in a mound next to her arm. She had no idea how long she stayed on the floor watching the sand pour through the light. The sand came for her—that she knew.

The sky had darkened again by the time she climbed out through the window and headed toward the superintendent's house. The wind increased with every footfall until it screamed in her ears; she didn't know where she was. She tried to head back to the buried house, but she couldn't find her way. The moment her feet left the sand, the wind erased her footprints. Storm clouds hurled overhead, and she stood on the beach near where she had first landed in the lifeboat. The island shook as the Atlantic rollers broke and crashed into the bar. Now that she had her bearings, she ran before the wind in the direction of the superintendent's house. A "fierce gust filled my dress," lifting her through the air and dropping her thirty feet away. She tried to stand and take another step, but the wind lifted her again and she flew another twenty feet with one step.

When she woke in the superintendent's house, she suffered from a terrible sickness that lasted for more than a week. She didn't care if she survived or not, but she did. Early in the spring, the schooner *Daring* arrived from Halifax to take the survivors of the wreck to the mainland, whence they made passage south to meet their families. Helen's father, still living, met her in Portland. He and everyone else in Vaughn had assumed that she was lost forever.

The sun rose and Phoebe wandered through the kitchen looking for breakfast and coffee as if she still lived here. There were no supplies, of course, and no power. She couldn't stand the silence, and she closed the front door behind her. Past the bell tower of the church, the blue sky seemed to vibrate. Halfway across the yard, she started to jog. The heels of her shoes crunched over last winter's road sand. At the car, she clicked open the door. In the driver's seat, she wrapped her hands around the plastic wheel and breathed in the smell of the rental, which was always the same no matter where she went. Looking up at Aunt Helen's room, she wouldn't have been surprised to see Michael come to the window and accuse her with his silence and his thin lips the color of pencil erasers.

She checked into a hotel in Augusta, where she stood with her mouth open in the shower letting the water pound her forehead. If her brother wanted to sell the house, he could fly out here and deal with it himself. If her father wanted the trunk and the other dusty stuff, he could fly out here and get it. She was finished.

By the time she dried her hair, flicked on the TV, and poured herself a cup of cheap coffee, she felt more rational. Mary had given her the names of two guys who would move the contents of the house to a storage unit, and she could tell them to haul it all to storage—every last stick. She and her parents could then split the cost of the unit for a year and deal with sorting the stuff next summer or just keep paying the fee for a while. Phoebe lay back on the bedspread and stared at the popcorn ceiling. The air conditioner hummed under the window. Somewhere inside the building, a cleaning cart with a broken wheel thumped down a hallway.

On her son Jacob's birthday last March—the last day Phoebe and Michael did anything with the kids together—they drove to the ocean. It was a cold day, and the low-hanging storm clouds seemed to merge with the gray water. The kids tried to pull Michael toward the surf. The more despondent he grew, the more they clung to him, but he told them not now and sat above the line of wet sand. Phoebe sat far enough from him that they wouldn't be able to hear each other without raising their voices. It had stormed the week before, and the waves rose high and broke.

The kids wandered the beach looking for sea glass, and suddenly Michael stood up and took off his shoes. She thought nothing of it at first, but then he removed his ball cap, windbreaker, shirt, and pants before walking into the water. His head dipped into the trough of a wave, and he was gone. She didn't breathe until his head splashed out of the wash, his back arched. Two bands of muscles formed on each side of his spine. He'd lost more than twenty pounds over the last six months, and his mannequin-thin shoulders seemed about to break. His lips turned purple. As he walked up the beach, Natalie ran up to him, and he flinched away from her. She stood with her arms at her side, watching her father trudge back to his spot in the sand.

The following month, Phoebe came home to find the back door open and no one home. He'd emptied his drawers, taken even the hangers from his side of the closet, and cleaned out his side of the cabinets in the bathroom. Anything that belonged to both of them he left behind, along with things that he must have decided he wouldn't need: skis, bike, CDs, suits, and ties. At first she wondered how he had transported everything—she drove their one car to work in the morning—but then she saw clothing overflowing from the trash bins around the side of the house. It looked as if he'd thrown away everything he owned.

She told the kids that Michael had gone to visit his mother up north in Sebastopol. Grandma was ill, nothing serious, Phoebe said, and he would be back soon. When his mother called Phoebe to ask why she hadn't heard from her son, Phoebe said Michael had flown to Mexico with an old friend for a few weeks. When her parents, who knew she and Michael were having trouble, asked about him, she told them the Mexico thing as well. As she lay in bed at night she thought of him out there, waiting for a ride by the side of the road. She imagined him anywhere, nowhere.

Several weeks before returning to Maine to empty Aunt Helen's house, Phoebe was driving down Waverly Street in Palo Alto when she spotted one of the water trucks that cycled through neighborhoods in the dry season to keep the trees and plants hanging from antique lampposts from drying out. A man in a blue city uniform stood in back of the tank, holding a three-foot nozzle up to a hanging planter. He looked from the nozzle to the planter and back to the nozzle as if he were performing a surgical procedure. He had grown a faint mustache, and his sunken cheeks seemed to have deepened the lines around his lips, but she recognized Michael. He didn't seem to notice her, even though she was driving the Toyota that he had insisted on buying with the silver color he had wanted, the bike rack he had installed, and the dent he had put in the bumper. She turned around, pulled up next to him, and rolled down her window. He turned off his sprayer, and his eyes narrowed as he leaned forward to squint at her. They remained like this for some time—she in the shadows, he in the light—but they didn't speak. It was too late, and had been too late for a while, to admit that she had left him behind. She had let him go under without offering any help. Thankfully, she thought as she drove away, she didn't have the kids with her.

Phoebe spoke to Mary about showing the house, should anyone ever want to see it, and she arranged for some men to haul the contents of the house to storage. She checked out of her hotel in the morning and drove to the airport in Portland. In a matter of hours, she arrived in California.

She had to pick the kids up from her parents' house on the way back from the airport. They had one day, Sunday, before their lives started again. The kids would go to camp, and she would go back to work.

Her father stayed on the patio as she greeted her mother in the front room. When Phoebe decided to give in to his rudeness and meet him in his troll-hole he didn't even rise. She leaned over to hug him and thought she heard him grunt. At this hour he usually drank a gin and tonic or a glass of wine, but he sat there with a clear glass of water in his hand. When she asked how he felt, he reached for the glass, brought it to his mouth, and merely touched the water to his lips without drinking.

"Where's the trunk?" he asked.

She thought about not answering him right away. She had stopped off at the house on the way to the airport in Maine to pick up the trunk. "Don't worry, I have it," she said, and he looked at her from under the overgrown ledge of his brow. He didn't ask her to carry it in, so she didn't offer. She wondered if he'd read all the logbooks and journals. Nothing in his watery green eyes betrayed his thoughts.

Phoebe's mother called her inside to help pack up the kids. Phoebe needed to hit the highway soon if she wanted to arrive home before the kids' bedtime. Also, she didn't want to fall asleep behind the wheel. She rushed the kids to say goodbye to their grandfather and loaded them into the car.

When she pulled into the driveway in Palo Alto, her son asked if his father was coming back.

"You said he would be back when you came back."

"No, I said that he *might* be back." She knew that she shouldn't have said that. "Do you know what the word *might* means?"

His closed lips moved back and forth across his teeth. He would need braces soon, and who would pay for that? She had yet to mention the extra-large storage unit in Augusta to her parents. Her father would be furious about the expense.

"I'm not stupid," he said.

"I didn't say you were stupid."

"You're lying," Jacob said, staring hard at her with the same scowl her father had just shown her on the patio. Technically, she had not lied, but, yes, she had lied. Somehow, her relationship with her kids—particularly with Jacob, whom she had begun, against her will, to see as a little Michael—had become legalistic.

"Tomorrow," she said, raising her voice so her daughter, who had darted back to her room, would hear as well, "we'll drive to the beach."

"I don't want to," Jacob said.

She settled the kids into bed and retreated to the back porch, which needed to be repainted or probably replaced, and sipped from a half-consumed bottle of white wine pulled from the back of the fridge. The full moon spotlighted her other real estate problems: dead grass with patches of dirt, a leaning wood fence desiccated by the sun, paint peeling off the garage. Inside: stained carpet, popcorn ceilings, hollow doors. She emptied the rest of the bottle into the back of her throat. She could still taste the cabin air of the plane—a problem no amount of wine could fix. She hadn't been drunk in a few years and wondered if she should open another bottle. Her cell phone rang, but she didn't answer it. An hour later it rang again and woke her. It was her mother, probably checking to see that they'd reached the house. She stumbled to the bedroom without answering.

The next morning, Jacob dutifully climbed into the backseat and folded his arms as he waited for his sister to assemble her backpack. Phoebe didn't have any food in the kitchen, and she didn't want to buy the kids chips at some gas station. She wove through town toward the opulent grocery store her father called the Arm and Leg, across from the coffee chain he called Five Bucks. Turning onto Waverly Street, she spotted the city watering truck again. A man stood behind the truck with the hose pointed at the base of a tree. Not Michael this time, but she slowed down.

"I thought we were going to the grocery store," Jacob said.

"We're going to eat poison from Circle K instead."

Phoebe followed the familiar route to the beach, through dry fields, live oaks, and over Skyline Boulevard—the same road her father had taken when they first moved to California. The kids fell asleep slouched against their seatbelts. Looking at them, she realized that she'd lived longer in California than in Maine, and now that she was selling the house the kids would never know the place where their mother, grandfather, and ancestors had grown up. They were California kids—whatever that meant.

She turned off the airconditioning and rolled down the window as they passed into the submerged light of the redwood forest. The road wound through the trees, whose tops vanished from sight in a thick canopy she had thought of as the earth's second surface. Lingering fog misted the windshield, and she wondered how the people who made homes in the mossy burrows tucked into the hills ever knew whether it was day or night.

When the bars registered on her phone, she pulled off the road, stepped outside, and called her parents. Her mother would have to find her glasses, which rarely happened before the call went to voicemail.

"What's wrong with Dad?" Phoebe said when her mother picked up on the fourth ring of the second call.

Her mother didn't speak for a few seconds; then she said, "He wants to talk with you himself."

"He didn't say much yesterday. Put him on the phone," Phoebe demanded, even though the last thing on earth she wanted was to talk to her father. She didn't want to explain that her husband might never come back, and she didn't want to talk about Helen's house in Vaughn.

"Not on the phone, Phoebe. And you stormed in and out of here like a tornado yesterday. It's the house, you know that. Give him some time. That's where he grew up."

"But he doesn't want to live there, does he? And he doesn't want to pay for it."

"We *can't* live there, and we *can't* pay for it. You're not being fair."

Phoebe hung up and got back in the car.

"What were you talking to Grandma about?" Jacob said after a few minutes.

"I thought you were sleeping."

"I was pretending to sleep," Jacob said with his eyes closed.

"People in our family do not divorce," her father had said to her at one point several months ago.

The road straightened and leveled, and the trees gave way to open fields and rolling hills. As they neared the water, the light struggled through the haze. In the rearview mirror, both Jacob and Natalie looked for a moment only vaguely familiar, like photos of her grandparents when they were children. She turned off Route 1 and parked at the same beach where they had gone for Jacob's birthday. Jacob trudged toward the sand with Natalie struggling behind under the weight of her backpack. Phoebe gazed at the sea as the kids headed south along the tideline to look for shells. Soon waves of heat and razoring light absorbed them, and she briefly panicked, but she hadn't lost them—she could still hear them.

Leaving her flip-flops in the sand, she walked to the water. A wave formed into the shape of a gaping mouth and collapsed in an explosion of spray. The wash reaching around her ankles and gathering strength around her calves pulled her toward the ocean. In the face of the next breaker, she saw a tumbling shape—an arm, she thought at first—but it was just seaweed.

A slouching dragon crept in her direction through a pool of heat floating above the sand. Jacob hunched in front and Natalie on the other end of a piece of driftwood. They lurched closer and dropped the log a few feet away.

"She wants to bring driftwood back," Jacob said and collapsed on Phoebe's right. Natalie continued to stand over the log.

"For the garden," Natalie said. She meant the garden Michael had once talked of starting in their barren backyard. Phoebe had no idea how her kids had dragged the log this far across the beach. Too long to fit sideways in their sedan, it probably weighed more than fifty pounds. "Can we take it home with us?" Natalie asked. Forcing herself to look her daughter in the eyes (at Michael's lashes and her father's green irises), Phoebe nodded.

"But first I want to talk to you guys about something," Phoebe said and felt the air escape her lungs. Nothing she could say to them about their father would make any sense.

As she turned back to the ocean, one of the tall rollers eclipsed the horizon. When the wave reached the height of its arc through the air, she began to tell her children about an island of blowing sand that swallowed ships whole—an island where horses stood as tall as buildings, where waves reached higher than skyscrapers, where storms lasted for weeks, and where a person with the wind at her back would fly thirty feet with one step. It was a place people could end up—an island where survivors waited for the drowned to walk out of the sea.

A Faithful but Melancholy Account of Several Barbarities Lately Committed

(2001)

John Jacobs Howland, Melissa Baraona,
Bridget Hutchinson Howland,
John Stoughton Howland

The day before my sister's pretend wedding, the family gathered in Maine for our annual meeting, at my grandfather's island house, so he could tell us how much of a disappointment we'd been. Dressed like a clam digger in rubber boots, filthy canvas pants, and an old sweatshirt full of pipe ash holes, he rose from his wing chair and levered himself to his feet with his cane. Stains extended from his collar to his knees because at mealtimes he used himself as a plate. Like other monarchs, he may have confused menace with majesty and mistaken the wary looks of his subjects, cowering in the wicker, for devoted affection. He delivered his judgment, not in words but through his leaky blue eyes, which lingered on each one of us before coming to rest on my sister.

"I am going to die," he announced, and lifted Julia, his corgi, into his arms. The wicker groaned. Of course he was going to die—at some point. He was ninety-four.

"Are you ill?" my aunt asked. With his flushed cheeks and one bony hand gripping the cane as if it were a sword, he didn't look sick. Just spiteful. Most years he accused us all of a failure of cheerfulness and left it at that.

"No, there is nothing wrong with me. I'm going to die, that's all. I am going to die on Saturday."

"But that's tomorrow," my sister said. "I'm getting married here tomorrow."

"You can go ahead and do whatever you want to," he said to the far side of the room. To where my fiancée, Melissa, stood next to a row of windows framing the Atlantic Ocean. "Who is that woman?" he asked.

Melissa raised her ink-black eyebrows and looked at me.

"Is that why there's a big hole in the ground?" my sister said, tipping her tennis racket west.

We'd all noticed the hole (three feet deep, a little bigger than a coffin) on the way up from the dock, but no one had mentioned it until now in the hope that ignoring it would fill it in.

"It's not even in the graveyard," my sister added.

"You're not putting me in the graveyard with all those people," my grandfather said to me for some reason.

"Those are our ancestors, and one of *those people* was your wife," Uncle Alden said.

"*Is*—*is* my wife."

"You're going to kill yourself on the day I get married?" my sister said. She and my father had distinguished themselves as the only two people to stand up to my grandfather. My father lived in Oregon and hadn't been back to Maine for a decade.

"Of course I am not going to kill myself."

"You can't just decide to die," my sister said.

"I can do whatever I damned well please!"

We all lowered our heads, except for my sister, who rolled her eyes.

"I am getting in that hole on Saturday. And someone," my grandfather added, nodding at me, "will cover me with dirt when I stop breathing."

"Why him?" Uncle Alden said. "Why does he get to bury you?"

"Because he inherits the house. As of Saturday, the whole thing belongs to him."

A great sigh seemed to rise from the floorboards, and Uncle Alden's head flopped forward. I felt dizzy and saturated, like someone who'd just downed eleven seltzer and lemons at a sports bar to prove he could sit there and not drink. At one time, before my first trip to COPE in Tucson, I'd spent every summer here on the island crammed into this eighteenth-century falling-down Cape with my sister and grandparents and cousins, all people I loved but also vaguely resented. I had always assumed that one of us—probably my Uncle Alden—would own it someday, but not me. I lived in Tucson and had no money.

"As of Saturday," my grandfather added as an afterthought, "whatever John says goes around here."

Unaccustomed to power, I didn't know if I should stand. Several cousins stormed out. A few climbed the stairs into what would apparently, as of Saturday, no longer be their bedrooms. I looked around at the old plaster, the whole house desperately clinging to the central stone chimney. A warehouse of colonial junk surrounded us: old paintings of people strangled by white collars on the walls of the parlor; a powder horn from Queen Anne's War on the sill; sea chests full of squirrel shit; calfskin log books detailing encounters with storms off Cape Horn and run-ins with the native people of Sin Jamaica. Along the hewn oak beam, over a hundred corks had been nailed to mark marriages, deaths, and New Year's Eves spent freezing by the fireplace.

Uncle Alden, who built uncomfortable chairs out of ash, which he offered at prices that successfully deterred their purchase, and my cousins—a couple of local teachers, a boat builder, and an organic farmer—had long feared that my sister, at first some kind of banker and now I didn't know what, would financially pick them off from her riverview condo in Manhattan and one day rebuild our sagging island house into a summer retreat for megalomaniacs. They would see my grandfather's announcement as part of my sister's scheme.

"Okay," my sister said, smiling. She raised her tennis racket and excused herself. For years she'd been the least-liked member of the family, but now that my grandfather had said he would leave the house to me, I figured the target might shift. Melissa caught my eye, and I signaled that I'd see her outside.

With everyone else gone from the room, my grandfather took out his pipe and clamped it between his teeth. The pipe was empty. He no longer smoked, not since he'd been diagnosed with emphysema fifteen years ago. He had probably not, as he claimed, cured himself of the disease, though as he bore down on one hundred, he had no trouble biking around on his motor-assisted adult tricycles—one for the island, one for town.

I had not grown healthier with age, either. I chose this moment to perform a self-check, which my fiancée, in her second year of graduate study in social work at the University of Arizona, had taught me to do. I could barely keep my eyes open. In response to stress, I always fell asleep. On a good day the medications I took rendered me as lethargic as a snake digesting a gopher. If not for my job and Melissa, I would've slept fourteen hours a day. I did not feel up to the challenge of whatever my grandfather and my sister had in mind for the weekend, and I had to will myself not to climb the stairs and lie down in my old room.

"You can't know what it's like," my grandfather said to me under his breath.

"What?"

"For everyone to want you dead."

"No one wants you dead," I lied.

"Bullshit," he said. "But I appreciate the sentiment." He tapped the empty bowl of his pipe on his palm as if to clear out yesterday's ashes.

I found Melissa outside talking to my braless cousin Bayberry, who leaned against my grandfather's island tricycle and raised her eyebrows. "Act One! Tomorrow, Act Two. Who is this man your sister's marrying? William St. . . . ."

"William Rollo St. Launceston," I said, reluctantly supporting the illusion that a real wedding would go down in the morning. No one else in the family knew that my sister and Rollo had already married at a secluded Maui beach a year ago. I hadn't been invited—no one had.

"That's a beautiful necklace," Bayberry said as she leaned into Melissa's personal space and squinted at her Our Lady of Guadalupe pendant.

"Thanks," Melissa said, and took a wary step back. I said goodbye to Bayberry, took Melissa by the hand, and led us down the trail. The island house was full, and the horsehair mattresses contained the bones of too many chipmunks, so I had reserved a hotel. In the shower at the Holiday Inn in Bath I could scald all the stupid things I'd heard today out of my brain. We reached the dock and boarded my grandfather's skiff to shuttle the quarter mile to the mainland. Sitting across from each other on bench seats, I was reminded, not for the first time, of the disconcertingly erotic fact that we were the same height, our shoulders the same width. Melissa had the softest skin on the planet, framed by her precision-cut bob feathering in the breeze.

On the way up the hill to the parking lot, Melissa touched my arm with the tips of her fingers and asked me if I was going to throw up. I had thrown up the month before, for no apparent reason, at a party hosted by a friend of hers. Ever since then she'd been waiting for it to happen again. Maybe I would; I didn't know. I turned to face the island, a low fir-topped mound ringed by jagged granite and dotted by shingled cottages. Every winter when I was young and my grandfather and I motored over from the mainland to fell a Christmas tree, steam poured off the ocean into the frigid air.

"It's mine," I said, a mostly false statement, and pointed to the island. "I mean, not the whole thing," I confessed. Though my ancestor John Josiah Howland and his wife Fear Chipman had swindled the island away from the Abenaki Chief Mowhiti-wormet, "Robinhood," in a 1640 land deal worth a hogshead of rum and twelve pumpkins, over the years each generation had lost a few acres. Now we owned only the farmhouse and the field sloping to the shore.

Melissa, not my real fiancée, not in the sense of someone who'd agreed to marry me, looked at my forehead. Did she know how I was feeling? That how I felt depended on how she felt? When I'd asked her to marry me two months ago, and she'd parried with "I need to think about that," I'd thought the trip to Maine might bring us closer together. And I *had* felt closer during the flight and the car ride up from Boston, so close that I had unconsciously shifted her answer into the "yes" box. Now, though, I didn't feel close at all. Maybe she would be impressed that I was—or soon would be—owner of the last few acres of the family homestead.

On the mainland, after we buckled ourselves into the Kia, I hit the gas, and we shot out of the parking space. Under stress I sometimes exhibited diminished motor control. I wondered if I was relapsing into what Melissa had once called a "disorganized attachment disorder," DAD, the description for which she'd read aloud from the DSM-IV. I did feel "systematically disregulated"; also, I felt "excessively friendly" and wished to continue expressing these feelings "in a syrupy, bizarre, ineffectual manner."

"We're not rich, you know," I said. I had jumped the reality track on the way up from Boston and now clung to the facts as a nostrum for all my natural impulses. "My sister and I grew up with my grandparents. My great-grandparents lost everything in the dowel factory in Lewiston. Anyway, you can't understand the family without understanding my grandfather." Neither a monarch nor (to his great relief, so he claimed) a *Kennebec Journal* "Local Person of Note," he was a retired high school teacher in Vaughn, a town twenty-five miles upriver from the island. To us he was the Old Man: the name, the dog, the cane, the Silver Star nailed to the wall in the back bathroom, and, of course, the title to the house on the island, the last thing of value owned by our family.

She put her hand on my knee. "You have boats," she said. "You are people with boats and an island with your name on it. Where I come from, people have broken cars." Melissa had grown up with a single mother in Douglas, Arizona, a place I privately thought of as a scary DMZ filled with guard towers, giant Border Patrol assault vehicles, and attack helicopters roaming the lunar border with Mexico.

"But we had broken cars, too," I said.

"Don't worry. I'm impressed."

"I don't want you to be *impressed*," I lied.

"This is my New England vacation. A break from the heat." Melissa traveled through time like an emotional space station that could go years without resupply. "Your eyes are weirdly geckoed," she said.

"I don't feel so good."

Melissa covered her left ear. "Stop shouting," she said. "I'm sitting right next to you." (I also sometimes lost control of "my volume," as Melissa put it.)

"Several weeks ago when I asked you . . . when I said I wanted to . . . when I told you I . . ." I was trying not to say "love" or "propose," two words she objected to. "I just hope—"

"To eat a lobster," Melissa said. "Me. *I* do. Before I get another boat ride." We stared out our windows for a while. "It's exciting that the house is really yours, John Howland. Of Howland Island."

This sounded better than John Howland, adjunct community college instructor. Back in Arizona, where no one gave a shit about New England, I could forget all that John Howland stuff, but here the name John Howland also belonged to my grandfather and his father, et cetera, in a more or less unbroken line of Johns going back twelve generations to the John Howland who accidentally fell off the stern of the *Mayflower* in a storm but thank God somehow managed to pull himself back aboard before landing at Plymouth so the rest of us could someday exist.

"Whenever I'm back here I feel as if I should be doing something more important with my life," I said.

"Why, because you think you're more important than people who do what you do?"

Melissa didn't understand, but I was encouraged by the way her gaze lingered on my jawline as we drove to Bath. When we first started dating, she claimed to admire my jawline. Now that I owned property, maybe we could have little John Howlands, what my grandfather had always expected. According to Melissa, I often felt so much that I had difficulty intuiting how other people felt, which didn't bother her, she claimed, because she didn't believe in codependency—in taking care of my feelings or telling me how to live—even though wasn't this the point of a relationship? To become less partial? The other night I'd dreamed that she and I were hiking in the Tucson Mountains when a giant tire—the kind used on mega-dump trucks—bowled over a rock, picked her up, and carried her surprised face down the side of a cactus-covered valley. I hadn't told her about the dream yet, probably because I thought she would say that the tire represented a wedding ring and that the dream expressed my rage at her lack of desire for a conventional commitment, which I thought I wanted but she claimed I didn't. At least not really.

In the morning, I motored us back across to the island. Melissa held our hotel coffees and asked me when she would get to meet my parents. My parents hadn't been invited to the wedding. I'd told her several times that when my sister and I were young my parents alternated between living in the house and with their back-to-the-land friends who "farmed" on a commune. After my mother ended up leaving for Mexico and my father for Oregon, my sister and I moved in with our grandparents. I hoped that reminding Melissa of my tragic story (that my parents had abandoned us) would keep me in the running as someone who had suffered enough for her to take seriously.

On the island dock, we sipped our coffee. Melissa gazed at the distant ocean with, I hoped, an Austenian longing for a life partner. All evidence to the contrary, Melissa longed for normal attachments. I *knew* she did. She had a tiny mole on her chin I liked to touch with the tip of my tongue while we made love. She pointed to a lobster boat loaded with nervous New York types leaving the mainland's dock and heading to another, larger, private dock my sister had arranged to borrow on the island.

"Is that a real lobster boat? Are there lobsters in that boat right now?" she asked. I answered that it probably was real even though half the workboats around the bay were fitted with lawn chairs rather than pot haulers. I pictured the two of us pulling up to the island dock in our own lobster boat (one that had been used for actual lobstering) with two kids sitting in the stern. We'd walk up to the house—*our house*—carrying those canvas tote bags summer people loved so much. In the fall we'd bake fish and play cribbage in front of the fire at night.

As we walked up the ramp, Melissa said, "Let me ask this: Do you think your sister will be mad that I didn't wear a dress?"

The idea of inheriting the house and the occasion of the wedding, fake or not, had gacked me out a bit. My thoughts unspooled faster than I could gather them up, and I was suddenly, unjustifiably elated and optimistic about the future. "I think I want us to move here and have a family." I stopped walking next to one of the graveyards filled with my ancestors.

Melissa seemed to be considering the pine trees and the field up ahead.

"This is my home," I continued. My eyelashes dripped. I hadn't realized how much I had missed it.

"You know," Melissa said with a grin that reminded me too much of how my sister had looked at my grandfather the day before, "you're not a nine-year-old."

"I need to talk about our relationship," I said.

"You mean the relationship you could just as easily have with a life-size cutout of my body?" She widened her eyes and dangled her arms in the air like a marionette. I didn't laugh. "Don't worry." She sighed. "I like you. You can be fun."

"I'm not *fun*," I said. I wanted her to understand I was angry, but I didn't want to take any responsibility for being angry.

"Not right now, you're not." She began walking again. "Look, John, in your own selfish way, you really care about people. And you can be more generous than me without meaning to. I admire that about you."

"You do?"

"My friend has a theory about why I like you." The apostrophe forming in the corner of her mouth forewarned me: either she was about to joke with me or say something depressing. Or both.

"You had something I never had."

"What's that?"

"A childhood." She stopped again. "And this is where it happened," she said, pointing to Devereux's Field. The grass leaned over in the breeze. When I turned back to her, she was no longer grinning. "It's exactly what I pictured. You want to live here?" she said, a small crack opening in her normally steady voice. "What're we going to do for money, raise sheep?"

What *were* we going to do for money? I had no answer. I could barely pay my rent in Tucson, and I had no job in Maine. I couldn't afford to maintain a falling-down island farmhouse or even pay the taxes. If I tried to sell it, no one in the family would speak to me again. If we moved here, Melissa and I wouldn't be able to feed ourselves, never mind a child. The house only had hay, seaweed, and horsehair for insulation against the winter storms.

"Do you think they will serve lobster at the reception?" Melissa asked.

My sister stalked out of the trees on the trail and, pointing at me, started speaking while she was still fifty yards away.

"I need you to talk to our grandfather," she said. "He's out there in the woods somewhere like a rabid animal. We can't have him crawling into that hole. You don't think he'll really get in the hole, do you? You are in charge of the Old Man." Now that she was standing before me, she poked my chest. To most of the family, my sister represented Greed, Ambition, Aggression. Striving constituted an unforgivable sin to those of us who believed ourselves chosen *a priori* and, therefore, beyond the indignity of scrabbling after the very things without which, of course, one found it difficult to feel chosen.

She looked over her shoulder. "Most of the family except the hippies have decided to boycott the wedding because they think we're pulling some kind of power move to take over the house."

"Did you say 'we' just now?" I asked.

"Everyone knows Mainwaring is actually gay, and Stoughton's already got two daughters and had the snip, I think. You're the last John Howland, and not only that: you're the last chance at *another* John Howland—not that I care. But if the Old Man gives the house to everyone, it will be sold because everyone but me lives on minimum fucking wage. My name should be John Howland for Christ's sake. That would solve a lot of problems." Like the Old Man, my sister had gone to Harvard. He talked slowly, with silent r's, while she (when she wasn't cursing like a fisherman) usually talked rapidly in lilting, hyperarticulate blocks of prose.

"Didn't your grandfather just give the house to John?" Melissa asked, and looped her arm around mine.

My sister, her bright blond hair feathering in the breeze, looked briefly surprised that Melissa had spoken. Though physically smaller, my sister radiated a sense of imminent invasion. "But he can't afford to pay the taxes on the house, can he?" my sister said. "So he'll need a partner."

When she moved to Manhattan—where, the rest of us were constantly reminded, the brightest people on the planet convened to congratulate each other—my sister lost interest in "Poison Oak Rock," as she called the island, because our Salem Witch Trials history didn't play well. But in the last few years, trends had shifted. Now Martha Stewart, born Martha Kostyra, didn't cut it in an authenticity-scarce environment. My sister, Bridget Anne Hutchinson Howland, eleventh great-granddaughter of persecuted religious fanatic Anne Hutchinson and twelfth great-granddaughter of *Mayflower* passenger John Howland, was a veritable *sui generis* snow leopard. I couldn't listen to my sister talk about her business (or about anything, really), but maybe she had a point about the house—I *would* need a partner. My sister and I would own the house fifty-fifty, and she would pay Melissa and me to be caretakers. It could work. We could blow insulation into the walls.

"When you talk to my friends during the wedding," my sister said with her eyes fluttering closed, "about yourself, say less. Professor Howland, maybe. Leave out your trips to rehab, the community college stuff, that you live in the third world of our own country." She looked at Melissa for a moment and rolled her eyes so quickly she might have only blinked. Then she pivoted and, legs scissoring, stalked across the field toward the house.

"I do feel sorry for you," Melissa said and put her hand on my back. "Having to grow up with that."

"She wasn't always this way," I explained. "Do you really feel sorry for me?"

"Not really," she said, which could mean she really did, or it meant nothing. We walked toward the house. It was a major concession for her to say she felt sorry for me, even as a joke.

138

To the right of the house, Uncle Alden and my cousin Main-waring stood with their hands in their pants pockets looking into the hole. A dog belonging to one of the wedding guests had fallen in. As far as I could tell, Uncle Alden kept promising to help but then continued to study the situation instead. The woman who seemed to own the dog repeatedly reached down but then, from obvious fear of falling in, backed away before she could grab the dog's collar.

"What did your sister say to the Old Man?" Uncle Alden whispered to me. Melissa pointed to where she would wait for me in the field and kept walking.

"Nothing."

"Bullshit," he said, still whispering. Uncle Alden pulled the tie out of his ponytail and tucked gray hair behind his ear. Strands fell beside his face and stuck to his lips. Uncle Alden had been doing a lot to take care of my grandfather, and he had clearly hoped he might inherit the house. Probably he should have.

"I've made a lot of mistakes," he said as he pulled me aside. I'd never understood what about me inspired family members to blurt out confessions. "It had something to do with psychological history. With *my* grandfather. We weren't supposed—we weren't *allowed*—to succeed at anything. Do you know what I mean?" I nodded, thinking of his uncomfortable chairs and the year he'd spent in the brig for refusing to cut his hair and go to Vietnam. Then I suddenly worried about the consequences of Melissa not having a good time and maybe not getting a lobster today. I looked around, but she had disappeared.

"I think the Old Man might've really lost his mind," my uncle said.

"It could be."

"He shouldn't be living in that big house in Vaughn by himself or coming down to the island alone. And this business with the hole in the ground and giving the house to you."

"What am I supposed to say? The house doesn't belong to me."

"He needs our help." Uncle Alden laid his fingers on my arm and left them there. I didn't know what to do—we didn't really touch each other in our family. "But he doesn't know how to ask for it," my uncle said. I thought of the story my grandmother had told of how my grandfather had jumped over the side of the Higgins boat at Omaha and advanced up the beach with the tide by keeping his head under the surface of the water except to come up for air.

"Okay," I said.

"So you'll talk to him about it?"

"Let's see what happens," I said and removed my arm from his grasp. Before he could touch me again, I strode recklessly toward a crowd of men in the field with wind-faring hairdos. Hired people in black outfits rushed around with trays of champagne. Except for the mosquitos, my sister had King Canuted the perfect conditions—bright blue sky with a few decorative cotton-candy wisps, the ocean covered with tinsel sparkles. Barren islands guarded the mouth of the bay, Hendricks Head Lighthouse right in the center of the view like a Wyeth painting.

I saw Melissa at the far end of the field, leaning against a tree and talking to a guy whose bald head shone in the light. Without eyebrows, he looked like a cross between a harbor seal and a penis. The guy before the guy she was with before me had been bald. I stopped in my tracks and watched her face and body language. Her curved lips (amazing lips!) pursed, and her canted hip bumped slightly against the clapboards.

My grandfather stood at the edge of the woods with his porkpie hat pulled low over his brow. The cane at the end of his extended arm looked like a metal rod supporting a statue. The way he held his head with his chin high and his shoulders squared reminded me of a picture I'd seen of him standing next to Theodore Roosevelt III—both of them with white face paint, blond wigs and long dresses—playing "chorus girls" in the Hasty Pudding club's 1934 production of *Hades! The Ladies!*

My uncle was right—my grandfather needed our help now, and I was the one he disliked the least. I waved to him and headed in his direction but immediately sensed someone stalking me. My sister's fiancé called my name. His friends called him the Rollocoaster; his ancestors, I suddenly recalled, had colonized Tasmania. Twenty years my sister's senior, he wheeled across the field on his springy legs. His pale, sparrow-thin thighs and incredibly erect posture flew the banner of his bright smile as he rushed to catch up with his projection of himself. I hoped he might sail right past me. Instead he took me in his arms, kissed my cheek, and in his unidentifiable accent asked how was I *keeping* and where were my *digs* these days?

He seemed pretty relaxed for someone about to perpetrate a fake wedding. Did Rollo know that I knew that the legal wedding had already occurred? I could picture his laser-shorn, hairless body gliding through the soft air above Maui's white sand beach. Even if I someday had money, I would never be happy enough to justify the expense of going there.

"I love that this place belongs to you now—the whole thing!" he said, beaming. "What are you going to do with it?" He gave my shoulder a solid squeeze. I'd never experienced the bonding between men who owned land. I stretched out my neck and surveyed the field. The house only came with four acres, but Rollo didn't know that. Or maybe he did.

"I think I'll live here—take up residence with Melissa," I said. I hadn't told Melissa that there was no electricity, no plumbing, no bathroom, but I could picture us drinking coffee by the kitchen window next to the stove as freezing rain sheeted over the glass. We'd pick apples from the orchard and bake pies and cobbler. Melissa would wear Irish sweaters and let her hair grow out.

"Your sister's talking about some kind of partnership with the house here. I like the sound of that. I think you and I have a lot in common. That's what your sister says. What do you think?"

I'd always wanted to have things in common with people, so I nodded.

"I'm pretty sure she wants to tear down that shack," he said, giving a quick nod toward the place my ancestors had built with nothing but an axe and their own hands, "or"—he air-quoted his pretend-bride-to-be—"burn it to the ground. Build something that isn't held together with mouse shit." He closed one eye and, aiming his arms so that I could take a look, too, framed the old farmhouse with his hands. "Something three stories? With cantilevered glass? Maybe steel on the north side. Something, you know, that takes advantage of the incredible light here. I'll text you what I have in mind."

The Rollocoaster peeled away. The ceremony was about to start. As I headed for the spot where I had last seen my grandfather, I felt a huge hole open up in my chest, and some unknown essential parts of myself spilled into the grass.

I couldn't partner with my sister, that carpetbagger. My grandfather wasn't even dead yet, and she was planning to torch the place. Even if I convinced her to save the house, she'd want to build a conference center next door, or a helipad, or there'd be product shoots for Martha Kostyra every other weekend. Rollo would be my master.

I smelled champagne in the sea air. I hadn't had a drink—or swallowed any unprescribed pills—in five years, but I also hadn't been to an AA meeting in over half that time. I rarely, if ever, thought about drinking or pills even when Melissa and I occasionally went to bars socially, which we sometimes did, with her friends to hear music.

Where was Melissa? Melissa, who resisted self-indulgence, who believed in kindness for people who deserved it and in justice for those who did not. When one of the men Melissa worked with at the shelter in downtown Tucson killed himself, she came home crying—the first time I'd ever seen her cry. After I cooked her supper and ran her a bath, I sat next to the tub while she soaked and eventually asked if she felt better. She shook her head. "It doesn't matter how I feel," she said.

As I passed by a table, my hand scooped up a flute of champagne and emptied the glass into the back of my throat. Before I realized what I'd done, I started to sway drunkenly, even though I wasn't drunk. I wasn't even pleasantly dizzy. Five years of sobriety down the drain. I half expected my head to explode or the grass under my feet to spontaneously combust. But the sky looked the same as it had a few minutes before. I picked up another flute. A fuse had been lit. Either I'd go looking for Oxy when we got back to Tucson, or I wouldn't.

Sipping, I took stock of the house, the glazing peeling off the window mullions. Feeling sick to my stomach, I poured out the half-empty flute. With the sound of the minister's voice following me, I circled behind the house to look for my grandfather. Along the forest floor, a new generation of trees had grown knee high where light filtered through the canopy. The dew clinging to the branches stained my pants as I ran my palm over the soft feathers of the needles. I remembered having walked this way many times, at every stage of my life. The tickling thrum that ran from my hand up my arm and along my back, the rich smell of pine sap and musty loam and salt air—other than the height of the trees, everything here had remained the same. I paused at the overgrown cellar hole, where one of my great-grandfathers had had his scalp removed by an Abenaki and where his two teenage sons, returning from fishing to find their father, mother, and younger brother lying dead, shot two of the Abenakis, hacked another to death, and chased off the one survivor. They turned in the three Abenaki scalps to the Massachusetts government and put the money toward materials to build a schooner.

I reached the far side of the house and spotted the caretaker's truck next to the grave my grandfather had paid someone to dig. As promised, my grandfather lay in the bottom with his arms crossed over his chest. Sitting on his stomach looking up at me, Julia licked her gray muzzle and eyeballed my empty hands. My grandfather's nostrils flared and his eyes shot open—pulsing blue crystals in bloodshot whites.

"John," he said. "Goddamnit!" He seemed angry with me, presumably for interrupting his death. "It's not working," he said and gazed up at me like a distressed child. He lifted Julia under an arm and tried to pull himself out of the hole with a pine limb. I offered my hand, but he slapped it away. When he started to fall backward, I wrapped my arms around his chest.

"Lift me up, for God's sake."

I planted my heels and struggled backward. We hovered over the hole for a moment and tumbled against a tree with our arms wrapped around each other, my face pressed against his cheek. He groaned as if I'd just stomped on his toe and scrambled away from me on all fours to lean against the caretaker's truck.

My grandfather and I lay on our sides facing each other. People in our field were quiet. The surf splashed with every other breath. The tendons and muscles in my lower back had seized, and a gash below my elbow bled onto my white shirt. I hadn't noticed the injury when my grandfather and I fell over, but I felt it now.

"I'm on a lot of medication," I confessed.

"Does it help?" my grandfather asked.

The wedding guests started to clap and leave their seats. As a way, I sensed, of not looking at me, my grandfather raised his bony hand and shaded his eyes to survey the crowd. Women in ankle-length dresses and men in dark suits spilled over the grass.

"Who are all those goddamned people?" he demanded.

"It's a wedding," I said. "Bridget ..."

"Yes. But who *are* they? Where the hell did they come from?" The muscles twisted under the creases and folds of his face, and I felt what he felt—revulsion at these strangers. "Jesus," he said, "what am I going to do?"

I turned away from him to face the beach, where four kids played on a pile of driftwood. Sandy-haired, somewhere between the ages of five and eight, they must've come with the guests. A woman my age, their mother or maybe a nanny, sat on a rock watching over them. My feeling that they trespassed had less to do with my inability to recognize them or the fact that the beach belonged to our family than with the sense that they threatened to eclipse my memories of being their age. They removed their shoes, rolled up their pants, and inched forward as a group into the shallows.

Wheels crunched over branches—my grandfather on his tricycle, slipping through the trees. I rose to my feet and jogged down the trail after him. With his cane stuck in the holster, he pedaled along the slope of Devereux's Field and turned left on the trail to the landing. Julia sat in the rear basket watching me slowly gain ground. As I pulled even with him, he looked through the trees to the west—in the direction of the car he wasn't licensed to use anymore, his home on Second Street in Vaughn where he'd grown up, and all the people he'd known since birth, most of whom were now in the ground at Oak Hill Cemetery.

"I don't want the house," I called to him.

"The house is mine!" he roared at me. In taking his eyes off the path, he almost veered into the ditch and had to slow to regain control. For a moment I thought he might stop, but then the tricycle sped up and bumped over the ruts, leaving me behind.

I recovered my breath and shuffled the rest of the way to the landing, where I found the tricycle ditched next to a tree. Across the channel, my grandfather tied up to the mainland dock and hefted Julia out of the skiff. The whole process took him much longer than it once had. He wrapped his arm around the cleat and pulled himself facedown onto the planks. Julia licked his cheek. When he didn't move for more than a minute, I thought maybe he had accomplished his goal after all. A moment later, though, he pushed himself to his knees and rose to his feet.

From my right, I heard Melissa call my name. She was standing on the boathouse's porch.

"I couldn't find you at the ceremony," she said, "so I went looking."

Her leather-soled shoes dangling from one hand, she seemed to float over the rocky ground as she drew near. Her skin pulsed around a mosquito bite almost exactly in the middle of her forehead. She was beautiful, perfect.

"Can we go to the reception now? I'm hungry," she said.

"Are you going to marry me?" I said, my voice rising in my throat. She grimaced and lifted my elbow to look at the cut; the bleeding had stopped, but my arm still stung.

Across the water, Julia barked at my grandfather's side. He took one excruciating step, rested over the railing with his mouth open, took another step, and paused to look back at me.

"Melissa," I said, my face growing hot, "what am I going to do?"

"You'll live," Melissa said as she let go of my arm and laid her cool palm against my cheek, "just like the rest of us."

Goat

(2013)

Anna Howland, John Jacobs Howland

At my uncle's funeral—if you could call it that—my cousin Anna grabbed my arm and asked me if I would help her spread his ashes near Castle Island on the Sassanoa River. But on the way, she said, we would have to deliver a goat. She stared at me with raised brows, waiting for an answer. Family and old friends of my uncle—who had read poems, performed songs, and recited memories of my uncle's youth—milled about the nature preserve, drinking wine where my uncle had daily practiced walking meditation. On the other side of the field, Anna's brother draped his arm over the shoulders of some guy who might have been a second cousin. They both held beers. Anna's brother spoke, while the cousin nodded at the grass.

"You mean sometime later?" I asked.

"No, I mean right now," Anna said.

"Okay," I said. As if I had just given her permission, she scooped the urn off the stump and shoved it into her backpack. Not even her brother seemed to notice as she bolted for the parking lot. I thought I had probably heard incorrectly, but there was in fact a goat standing in the back of her truck chewing on the end of a branch that hung down from above. "Natalie," Anna said, gesturing to the goat. She started the engine and hit the gas as if we had just robbed a 7-Eleven. On the road, she explained about the goat, which had shown up at her job site near Robinhood Cove. She had worked in a law office for a while, she said, but was now a carpenter and caretaker for summer houses. I hadn't seen her or any of the family in some time—I hadn't been back to Maine for over five years.

"The goat lives on Castle Island." She looked in the rearview mirror and held her hand out the window. Warm, late August, the kind of day that would have found us playing on the raft in the cove when we were kids—though I was ten years older than Anna. We hadn't been kids at the same time.

"Everyone's happy you came back for the funeral," she said. I wanted to ask if her brother would be happy that we had stolen the urn. Anna's parents had been divorced for at least ten years, and her mother hadn't come to the funeral, but other cousins and relatives now searching the field for the urn would wonder where Anna and Uncle Alden had gone. Having absorbed my fill of amateur sonnets and the banjo, I was just happy to be elsewhere. My flight left in the morning; I welcomed the idea of a boat trip.

According to Anna, there was a guy and his girlfriend on Castle Island, where the goat lived, using the cabin there to hide from the feds. Drugs, Anna said. The story of these people on Castle Island, these hardened criminals using a goat for cover, made no sense. I didn't believe the people existed at all. I still didn't really believe we had run from the funeral with the urn. I looked through the rear window to make sure there was a goat in the bed of the truck. There was. If my wife, Mary, had come with me (she couldn't have come—our son, Justin, started soccer camp today), she would've talked me out of getting into a truck with my cousin and a goat. When I was away from Justin, even for a day, I sometimes felt as if I would never see him again, and a fist squeezed in the center of my chest. To distract myself now, I looked at Anna.

I remembered from my occasional visits to Maine when Anna was in her twenties, and her hippie parents still called her Bayberry, that she had dropped out of several colleges and always seemed stoned. She'd wanted to study bio touch or massage therapy. She'd even mentioned, if I remembered right, massage therapy for horses. With gray hair and lines around her mouth, she now looked exactly like her mother at the same age. We were both old.

"They're still there, these drug dealers?" I asked, not caring if the whole story was made up.

"I don't know. Probably not. Maybe." Some truth was usually mixed with bullshit in our family; separating the two required too much energy. Anna told me about her last job before deciding to work for an old friend who was a carpenter. She'd been an office assistant for Mr. Ingersoll, the lawyer in Bath. I had known one of his kids in school.

"In case anyone made the mistake of underestimating his importance," she said, "the degree from Bowdoin hung on the wall to the right of his desk. The glass had fallen out of the frame, and man, I was tempted to lean over and scribble graffiti next to the Latin."

When Mr. Ingersoll worked, he hummed loudly. According to him, he couldn't control it, which Anna didn't believe.

"It really seemed like the kind of noise you made on purpose, especially in a small office with only two rooms. To try to muffle the noise, he started stuffing his mouth with typing paper, which he chewed as he hummed. When I couldn't sleep at night, I heard his mouth macerating the paper. I couldn't take it anymore."

At the Robinhood boatyard, Anna reached around behind her seat, pulled out an old wooden cane with a curved handle, and set it in my lap. The cane, one of the few things I'd hoped to have from my grandfather, had vanished from his house the day after his funeral. I had always suspected Anna's father, Uncle Alden, of taking it.

"Here. My father didn't want you to have this," she said. "Those were some of his last words."

"You're kidding me."

"Sort of. He love-resented you," she said with the kind of smile I'd only seen where I'd grown up. A kind of tyrannical yoga-face pose of false cheer. "I don't want the cane. You may as well have it."

I thanked her and eased out of the truck to lean on the cane. In not too many years, I might need it. Anna asked me to hold the rope attached to the goat while she looked for the boat keys. Eyeing me warily from its left eye, the goat blinked. Or winked. A tinkling sound alerted me to the leather collar. *Natalie,* a tag said, confirming that part of Anna's story.

She found the keys and led the goat down the ramp to the dock. The goat glanced at me suspiciously, but she looked at Anna the way my dog in Oregon looked at me right before his suppertime. I carried the cane in both hands like a submachine gun. With the goat tied to the center console, we sped out of the harbor toward the Sassanoa River, past Lower Hell Gate and the Boilers to Castle Island. I hadn't been this way since before my grandfather died; the number of houses along the shore had doubled in that time. The air was salty and balmy. A mile farther upriver, we passed through pockets of cooler air. Anna nosed the boat up to the small beach, cut the engine, pulled up the prop, and threw the small anchor onto the sand. Then she started to take off her shoes and pants, leaving on her underwear.

"What are you doing?" I asked.

"Don't want to get my jeans wet." She smiled. "Come on. Nothing we haven't seen before."

It took me a moment to realize she probably referred to the times all the cousins went skinny-dipping when we were young. In the summer we all stayed with my grandparents on an island downriver where the family used to have a house until a few years ago. I took off my shoes and pants, leaving on my shirt and underwear, and hopped into the icy water. I tried to coax the goat overboard, but she stomped her hoof as a warning for me to back off.

"She must be afraid of the water," I said.

"She can't be that afraid. She keeps swimming ashore to get off this island."

"So you've brought her back here before?"

"The people who own the island—they're from Massachusetts—they want the goat out here. They think she eats the poison oak."

"Not the drug dealers?"

"No," she said. "They're squatters."

When she started to lift the goat out of the bow, I insisted on helping her even though Anna was five foot nine and probably stronger than I. If she fixed cottages on the islands, she would have spent a lot of time dragging lumber out of boats. We set the goat on the beach, and all three of us stood with our feet in the sand. Anna still had a narrow waist, while I had a belly concealed under my shirt and was balding. The last time we had gone swimming as a family, she had probably been ten and I twenty. Back then the whole family lived in the town twenty miles or so upriver, and all my cousins had been like siblings.

"Come on," she said. "I'll show you the cabin." I followed her up the trail and wondered, if her story had any truth to it, if we should be wandering around the island with drug dealers nearby. The shingles of the cabin had worn gray, and most of the glazing from the windows had fallen out. The people from Massachusetts couldn't have come up very often. I followed her inside and found nothing at all except a single empty coffee can in one corner, a broom in the other. Some smell pinched my nose. Either the mildew and wet wood or the damp earth under the floor.

"You should have seen it before I mucked it out," she said.

We returned to the small porch, and she sat down on the boards and leaned against the railing with her legs pulled up. I sat down opposite her. Hearing a rustling and scratching in the bushes next to the cabin, I thought of the goat's horns, wiry hair, and small eyes, and then the goat appeared at the foot of the porch stairs.

"I am glad to see you," Anna said. "And I'm not that glad to see many people these days."

I didn't have any hard feelings about my cousin—I wished her well—but I really didn't want to hear why she was happy to see me or not so happy to see others. Close proximity to family loaded me with resentment and guilt in roughly equal proportions. I already regretted leaving the nature preserve, where collective dissociation had seemed like the social contract.

"When we were young," she said, "it felt like there was something unique about us. Like we were something special. The *Howlands*."

"We're not," I said, "something special."

Anna frowned, and I wanted to say that at times I still thought of certain moments—our grandfather, holding forth during cocktail hour on the brilliance of *Zorba the Greek*. But what she called our *specialness* had almost killed me. There was no way of explaining that to her without resorting to the kind of melodrama I had spent these last years trying to avoid.

The goat started nibbling on my shirttails. With her little goatee, she looked a lot like my junior high gym teacher, Mr. Dawson, who had a way of letting you know with a quick glance that he was disappointed in your athletic abilities. The sunlight shone through the gaps in the spruce. Grateful that Uncle Alden had died of cancer in the summer rather than in the middle of mud season, I raised my chin to the sun.

"My father with his stories of the brig during Vietnam," Anna said, "sent there because he wouldn't let them cut his hair—he taught sociopaths to play chess. And your side. Your mother went to Mexico, your father joined some commune on China Lake, another in Oregon, and you moved in with Grandma and Grandpa—I was jealous of that. It felt like you got a part in the play, while I was some kind of understudy on the other side of town."

"My father's still in Oregon," I said, "but he lives in our garage now. I fixed it up with new carpeting and a minifridge. It's nicer than my house." I had explained that my father was too ill to travel to the funeral—he'd had bypass surgery a month before—but in reality he had said he couldn't bear to see everyone.

"It was Grandpa at the center of it," Anna said. "Omaha Beach. Whatever he did to get that Silver Star that used to hang on the wall in the back bathroom of the island house. And the hurricane."

She was right about that story—how he saved everyone on a schooner during Hurricane Carol. Waves fifty feet tall. Everyone cowered in the cabin of the schooner, while he ran on deck to tie down the storm jib. When he tried to secure the boom, it swung loose and he careened over the water. I knew every word and every moment of that story.

"And the time he and his college roommate played volleyball with Herbert Hoover."

"Yeah," I said, drawing a hard but arbitrary line in my head, "that never happened—probably." I thought of the story of how my grandfather hit an inshore reef going wide open in the skiff. The boat landed on the rocks, and he landed, sitting up, in a Southport Island woman's flower garden. I hadn't been with him that day, but I could picture how the woman, Caroline Sprague, fell out of her chair and sprained her arm. I could see her scowl as she sat in the passenger seat, driven to the hospital in her own car by the enormous man who'd fallen from the sky.

There were other stories. The only thing we knew for sure about the Old Man was that he had taught English at the high school for about forty years.

"And my father," she said. "He lived in a house in Cambridge for a while—supposedly. When my mother wasn't around, he told me about cooking spaghetti with Robert Lowell."

A mosquito landed on Anna's knee, and, leaning over to slap it, I felt myself softening. No reason for me to be so hard on her—she just wanted someone to talk to. The tiny plastic imp in the glass bottle of my soul thrived at ridiculing my family, who I imagined had made me feel unappreciated and misunderstood.

"And despite all that—or maybe because of it, I don't know—I felt growing up as if there was something wrong with us. Do you know what I mean?"

I didn't say anything, but I did know what she meant. When our grandfather told the story of our first ancestor in America tumbling off the *Mayflower* and almost drowning, he meant to warn us. Uncle Alden had once joked that the family motto should be "Keep your head down and stay out of the water."

"I miss the drama," Anna said, squinting at the water stretched out before us. "I don't feel like I'm part of a *story* anymore."

"I don't miss it," I said.

But I thought of the day each winter when my grandfather and I rowed over to the island where we once owned a house so we could cut down a Christmas tree from the woods. The last time we went I must have been thirteen, and I was wearing L.L. Bean boots that were at least a size too small. Saying they cost too much, my mother had refused to buy me new ones. Until the next year, she said, the rubber would expand around my foot. I walked with my toes balled into knots. Steam poured off the ocean into the frigid air. Snow had recently fallen, and the branches of the spruce bowed under the strain as we walked up the path. Holding the axe in one hand, my grandfather went up to one tree after another and shook free the snow to see if the shape and height would do for the parlor of their house on the mainland. He shook several short, chin-high trees just for the fun, it seemed to me, of shaking them. I shook a couple, too. My grandfather's wool hat was covered in snow, and his gloved hand brushed against the branches of every tree in reach as if he were greeting a crowd of fans.

"They're all gone now," Anna said, "at least from my life. Those giants. Grandpa, Grandma, my father, your parents. You're the last one."

"Me?" I looked at her. "You're kidding."

"The golden boy out there in San Francisco working in the theater."

I thought she had to be talking about someone else.

"I only lived in San Francisco for a short time, working in a bar, and we were whacked out on speed putting on plays about nuclear annihilation in an old warehouse."

"That's exactly what I mean!" she said and laughed.

"No one came to see us. Then I went to rehab in Tucson and spent some time on a psych ward. Now I teach history at the community college in Eugene. What's romantic about that?"

"But you like it out there. You never come back. We've never even met your wife. Mary? And—don't you have a kid?"

"Justin's seven. And I do like it out there. The only real difference is that we have spruce trees here, and they have Douglas fir out there."

"I bet you're a good teacher."

I had no idea, really, if I was any good or not. I was grateful for the job—mostly grateful for the kind of work I didn't have to do. If you have the luxury of studying or teaching history, then the primary lesson of the material is gratitude. Most people in human history enjoyed no luxury at all.

"Do they use Doug fir for framing out there?"

"I think they do."

She nodded, and we sat in silence for several minutes. Then Anna said, "I'm pregnant." She rested her hand on her belly. I tried to calculate her age—she might be close to forty, the age of my wife when we had Justin. A year and a half later, when we tried for a second, it was too late.

I congratulated her. "Is there a father involved?" I immediately regretted asking.

She sighed. "There was a guy involved. Not now. And with my mother living in North Carolina and my dad gone . . ."

"I am sorry about your father," I said to her for the second time that day.

"Everyone's gone—except my brother, and he lives in Boston."

"That's not far away."

"He never comes back up here, and we don't have much to talk about. I think he spends most of his time in sports bars hitting on college girls." She tossed her hand in the air. "What's the point of having a kid?"

"What I often wonder is: what would be the point if I hadn't?"

"I guess I always thought you of all people would move back."

"I have a good job. We have a house and a mortgage—and it turns out our grandparents were wrong. People are basically the same everywhere. Not everyone goes haywire on the West Coast." I asked her if she planned to have the baby, and she shrugged.

"I wish you lived here," she said.

"My father lives with us, and Justin keeps us busy. We're busy," I said, making excuses for not keeping in touch or visiting. "We have a dog."

"Do you think I should have the baby?"

"Why are you asking me?"

"I guess I don't have that many people I can ask. And you were like Grandpa when I was young. You were one of the giants."

"I don't know what to say."

"I'm afraid," she said, "to do it alone. Because that's what I would end up doing."

I wanted to be able to encourage her, but instead I asked if there were actually drug dealers living on the island. Or had that been a story to lure me out here and pepper me with questions? She ignored my sorry joke.

"With my father gone," she said, "I feel like I have to have the kid no matter what." From the way her voice wavered at the end of the sentence, I thought she might be crying.

"Shouldn't your brother be with us," I asked, "to spread the ashes? It's none of my business."

"My father told *me* to do it," she said gruffly. "He didn't tell my brother to do it. Just me." She stood and brushed dirt off the backs of her thighs. "He said Hockomock Bay was the only place he was ever happy at all—when he was a kid swimming up here."

"You should have the baby," I said. I shouldn't have spoken, but I wasn't going to take it back. She nodded. We walked back down the trail toward the beach, and I thought of what it would be like to hear that your father had never been happy while you were alive. My parents had seemed less restless in the last ten years. My father liked sitting in his lawn chair outside the garage and drinking craft beer. He gave Justin the thumbs-up when he ran by. My mother flew up from Mexico to visit us once a year.

We reached the beach where we had landed, but the boat was gone. Anna glared at the anchor and the line trailing into the water.

"I threw out the anchor. I guess I didn't tie it to the boat," she said.

Our clothes were in the boat. I scanned the water downriver until I thought I saw the white hull turning in the current, ferrying the boat toward the rough water of Lower Hell Gate and eventually the open ocean. "I see it," I said, my heart pounding.

"Yeah, me, too. Shit." She looked toward the mainland to the west, maybe a quarter mile away. No houses lined the shore directly across from us, where a granite cliff rose above the water, but I could see docks up and down the river.

"It's summer," I said. "People are around." I was short of breath, and my fists clenched. Calm down, I told myself, no crisis. "We'll be rescued or we'll swim for shore and find help." It didn't matter what I said to myself. We stood on an island watching our only mode of transportation being whisked away.

"My father's in the boat," she said and sounded for a moment like the girl I remembered on the island in the summer—my younger cousin at the supper table asking to run down to the beach with me and the others.

"I'll go," I declared and shed my shirt.

"I'm younger," she said, adding, without meaning to be cruel, "I'm in better shape."

"You're pregnant," I said and eyed the boat slipping farther away with every second I waited. I sensed the goat somewhere behind me, bothering the ground amidst the poison oak. When I turned around, she seemed to be laughing at me, though she might have been chewing.

I dove in and immediately felt like screaming from the cold shock. At first I managed what I thought must have looked like a panicky crawl, but in rougher water I soon slowed. The cold wasn't enough to kill me, just enough to bore into me and form a hard layer, a skin inside my skin. I thought of Justin running across the soccer field in his green-and-yellow shorts. His pale legs were so thin, I was afraid they would snap when he went for the ball. Wanting to run circles around him all day, putting myself between him and the world, I worried I was like a cloud blocking his sunlight.

The current hit me and pushed me south toward Lower Hell Gate, where the high chop and twisting water would pull me under. I had flown all the way back here for a funeral just to drown while returning a goat to its summer residence—an allegory my grandfather would have told about the dangers of moving west. Of course he hadn't been worried about me as much as himself. What would happen to him without an audience? I never found out because I wasn't here. I had just moved to Oregon when he flew over the handlebars of his electric tricycle and ended up in the hospital with broken ribs. When I called the hospital, I told him I would get on a plane right away. "It's not that kind of thing," he told me from his bed. I should have ignored him—he was ninety-seven. That night he had a heart attack but survived. The next day he got out of bed, pulled the tubes out of his arms, pushed Uncle Alden and a nurse out of the way, and stormed down the hall. He died, I was told, five feet short of the front doors.

As I slowed to a dog paddle, I pictured my pale, bloated body washing up at the mouth of the Sheepscot Bay, my mouth open and eyes plucked by sand crabs. Found by tourists, I'd be hauled off to some metal slab, and my family would have to fly out. My mother and father would have to get on planes. Justin would see me as no father—no person—wants to be seen: fat, pale, naked, a fish on ice. I started to gasp. Swallowing a mouthful of saltwater, I thrashed my way into a rope and grabbed at the handle of a lobster buoy as if it were a raft. I kept dipping beneath the surface and watching as the light fractured above. Only when I stopped fighting was I able to float onto my back and breathe. With my ears submerged and my lips above the surface, I listened to the water flowing under me. A white cloud in the shape of a cupcake inched across the sky.

When I raised my head and looked around, I saw that the boat had drifted out of the channel onto the mud flats and was wedged against the bottom only twenty-five yards away. I wasn't in the current at all but in an area of open flat water that grew shallow along a marshy shoreline. By the time I dog paddled to the hull, I could touch bottom. Though I had a hard time pulling myself over the side (at home I exercised only to walk the dog), I still had enough energy to stand and wave to Anna. She waved back with her whole left arm, then both arms, swinging in the air. I was still alive. We were both still alive! I yelled across the water that I was coming to get her, but the wind had picked up. I doubted she heard me.

The keys rested in the ignition of the console, the urn in the backpack on the floor of the boat next to my grandfather's cane. I could push off the mud with the oar and pick Anna up in less than a minute. For the moment, though, I sat behind the wheel, looked across the water at my cousin, and thought of hanging out on the back deck with my family when I returned home to Oregon. I would slice up a cold watermelon while Mary passed out paper towels. They'd want to know about my trip, and I'd be eager to tell them the story. As soon as I let slip the part about the goat and the urn, the tale of how I'd almost drowned as I boldly swam through rough water and gale-force winds to rescue my pregnant cousin would begin to tell itself. Before I even finished, Justin would ask me to stop and go back to the beginning. He'd want to know what I'd been wearing, about the time of day, the temperature of the water, the number of sharks. Just like me at his age, he'd want us to go over and over what had happened until he knew every detail by heart.

Wintering Over

(2014)

Charlotte McKinney, Nathan Bradford

They were going to Maine because Nathan had recently walked out on a book contract and returned the modest advance after declaring that he had nothing left to say. His editor and longtime friend had seen part of the new manuscript and had told Nathan that he had betrayed his own vision, a statement that Nathan felt betrayed their friendship. He said he needed to reinforce his foundation. They had decided, he reminded her, to wait a few more years before having children, so they had time for an adventure.

When he first mentioned spending the winter in Maine, Charlotte had been excited, picturing the rough coast, fir trees, mountains, and clear rivers of the northern landscape she had seen in the Travel section of the *New York Times* and read about in scenes from Nathan's own fiction, mined from his boyhood trips to summer camp. She had hoped the beauty would inspire her own work in new directions and had planned to bring her potter's wheel. She felt optimistic, so it was a disappointment to hear Nathan say that he no longer cared about beauty—not since the failure of his last project, which had ended not so much with his walking out on a contract as with his book walking out on him.

"Beauty like that is dangerous," he said when she suggested they consider one of the places she'd heard about, Bar Harbor or Boothbay, with grand old houses and sweeping views. "It's made me complacent, aesthetically lazy."

Having grown up on military bases around the country and lived until eighteen in the squat, drab houses Nathan had once described in a story as "toad-like," Charlotte felt she would never be surrounded by enough beauty.

"I'm not sure this town Vaughn is a nice place—in fact, I am pretty sure it isn't—but that's the point, you see? A defunct mill town—also an ice and granite town—that hasn't seen prosperity since they made shoes for Union soldiers in the Civil War. I've been reading about it. In the 1700s, it was one of the richest towns in New England. Logs driven down from up north were milled on the banks and loaded on ships along with granite. Benedict Arnold camped there on his way to attack Quebec. It does have old houses, and it is an old town; it just isn't a *tourist destination.*"

"Fine," she said.

"Are you sure it's fine?" He looked at her, and she kissed him on the head.

"I just want you to start working again," she said, offering one true statement.

Charlotte had hoped to arrive in Maine before the leaves had fallen, but she and Nathan didn't descend into the Kennebec Valley until late fall, long after the trees this far north had shed their colors. Following the river inland from the sea, they passed, every five to ten miles, a small collection of soporific storefronts and three-story brick and clapboard captains' houses surrounded by the tangled fingers of bare oaks and maples.

The real-estate agent met them at a colonial with fireplaces in every room. The house, the "old John Howland House," according to the Realtor, had been owned by the Howlands since its construction in the 1700s. "They haven't decided what to do with it yet. The family removed a lot of the oldest items, but some of the furniture is as old as the house. So you two are going to winter over?" the Realtor said in his Maine accent, and Charlotte winced. Nathan tended to absorb regional dialects, and, whether on purpose or not, mimic them. "Yes, yes, we'll be wintering over," Nathan answered with a smile.

Charlotte could set up her wheel in any of the downstairs rooms. She ran her fingers over the ripple of a leaded glass window and turned to watch Nathan step into the next room, rubbing the layers of his recently cut hair above the nape of his neck. From the back and except for his gray hair, she could imagine what he must have looked like when he was a college senior. His jaw was as smooth and narrow as in the photos of his years on the college newspaper, though his skin, like his hair, had grayed early, lending a certain gravity to a man who otherwise remained a boy. In the eight years she had been with Nathan, she had noticed her body aging: the lines around her eyes and mouth, a slight settling around her waist. It seemed now as if Nathan might stay just as he was forever, out of stubbornness, allowing her to catch up and pass him by.

She asked the Realtor how much the house rented for and was surprised to hear it was a fraction of what a one-bedroom would cost in their neighborhood in Hastings.

Raspberry and strawberry bushes overgrew the backyard, reaching through wild grass to what had been a vegetable garden. Heated by a wood-burning furnace, in addition to a woodstove in the kitchen and a Franklin stove in the parlor, the house would demand their attention through the winter, the Realtor warned. In what must have been the dining room, the floor sloped, and at a point where one of the foot-wide pine floorboards had split, Charlotte could see into and smell the dark basement.

"The house was used in the Underground Railroad," the real-estate agent said. "In the basement you can see where there was a tunnel that used to lead from here down to the factory."

"How many cords of wood does the furnace burn in the winter?" Nathan asked the Realtor. He had already started dropping his r's.

"Depends on the winter. Maybe ten."

As Charlotte tried to picture Nathan rising at 5 in the morning to descend those basement stairs to feed the furnace, she studied the cracked yellow linoleum that curled at the edge of the kitchen. She often thought of the torture Nathan endured for his writing as picking at a scab. She had once wanted to be a writer herself and had read about and listened to gossip about writers with a level of eagerness that could only be sustained by not knowing any.

She had known about Nathan from his books before she'd seen him, and when she first saw him, it was from a distance. As with anything one ever thought of as beautiful, or anything about which one could be nostalgic, she had no regrets. Nathan had been criticized for being nostalgic in his work, but she had always loved his ability to find certain ordinary things (hammers or saws in junk shops, farmland) fascinating because he had known them in his boyhood.

That Nathan had recently identified any kind of boyishness, sentimentality, nostalgia, or beauty as characteristics he would now seek to shed in this town, a place that seemed to have been forgotten even by the people who still lived there, did not worry her too much. He liked to talk about the pain of transformation— of their relationship, of himself as a writer and a person, and particularly of his characters. Prone to sudden, self-flagellating lows, Nathan enjoyed his temporary discomforts on his own terms. In the end he always more or less returned to where he had started.

They took the house on a month-to-month basis, and as he talked with the Realtor about the rent and the delivery of firewood (he kept using the phrase "Do you know a good man?" when asking about carpenters and mechanics), she decided to take a walk up the street.

Charlotte had a feeling that she had often experienced when she was young and she and her parents arrived in a new place. She had gone from dreading those moves to anticipating the excitement, in no small part, she knew, because her skinny frame had filled out and her round face had thinned. Her skin pricked under the gaze of a whole lunchroom or classroom drawn in her wake. She knew how to hold herself apart, eating alone with her chin held high and waiting for them to come to her. When they did, she sometimes talked about places she had seen on the globe in her bedroom. Places no one she knew had ever been to.

At his reading where they first met, Nathan eventually crossed the room after the rest of the audience had gone home. He wanted to know if she had enjoyed the reading. She watched his lips. That night he asked her dozens of questions, but he never asked her whom she had come to the reading with. In fact, she had gone to meet a boy she had been dating who didn't show up, a fan of Nathan's who had been raving for weeks about his writing. This boyfriend wanted to be a writer, presumably one like Nathan. Now the boyfriend practiced law, and she lived with the writer he'd wanted to become.

Charlotte thought she knew Nathan's real problem: he was forty-eight years old and no one read his books. Not literally no one, of course, but basically no one, as he liked to say. Aside from grants and fellowships that he seemed to almost resent, he'd never made real money from his work, and even though he sometimes took teaching jobs, he had always seen teaching as an undignified way for writers to earn a living. Nathan was respected, he was reviewed, he went to Yaddo, he gave readings at universities where his friends taught, but he had, she suspected, come to the conclusion (either consciously or unconsciously) that his life's pursuit was a little self-centered and pointless. Did barbers, dentists, lawyers, Realtors, accountants, and carpenters feel that their life's pursuits were somehow grand? No. Why should Nathan be an exception? He talked about what she saw as the central fact of his life (and now her own): his grandmother had left him a small pile of money, which Nathan's cousin managed from his corner office in lower Manhattan. The connection between his good fortune and the burden of self-identity never seemed to occur to him.

Snow fell two and a half weeks after they spent their first night in the house. Nathan descended the cellar stairs to feed the furnace as he did every morning at 5:30 so she could have a hot bath. No shower in this bathroom, only the cast-iron tub. By the time she heard him coming back up, the road sloping down to Water Street had vanished under a clear white blanket. She slipped outside in her bare feet while the bath filled. The snow didn't even seem cold melting under her soles. She left black prints over the pavement as she walked down the street, stopping just beyond the tracks and turning to see Nathan in the window of the second floor, smiling at her from his writing room. She had the familiar feeling that in his eyes she was a character who had the right appearance for her role. She gave him the finger, but even this seemed scripted; he laughed and ducked back into the shadow of the room where he'd set up his typewriter. He wrote all his first drafts on the typewriter and later entered the material into the computer. His process.

Her feet ached in the hot water of the tub. She didn't linger but dried off, dressed in the cold bedroom, and headed downstairs with a sense of vigor to her workroom, her "studio," in what had been the dining room. She started the electric wheel, listened to the whir of the engine, and watched the grooves of the metal disk spin. For some reason, she hesitated to begin, but finally she dug her hands into the bag of wet clay. Outside, the snow fell pleasantly through the gray air. Her fingers slid through the clay and squeezed what felt like a knotted muscle she meant to disentangle into a bowl. The sun broke through the low-lying clouds over the river, and she was just starting to fall into a rhythm when she heard a thundering crash from the back of the house. At first, she thought the train had ground to a halt in the middle of town, as it had the other day for some reason, but the noise had come from the opposite direction. When she looked out the back window, she saw an enormous dump truck pulling away from a pile of unsplit wood covering the car lot. The pile stood at least nine feet tall. She hadn't quite recovered from this shock when the back of an even bigger truck came in around by the old vegetable garden and left what seemed to her enough wood to build a fort. Nathan walked outside and stood between the piles with his hands on his narrow hips.

The trucks rumbled up the hill, leaving Nathan standing alone looking at one of the piles. The tops of his bare hands turned purple. She thought about bringing his hat and jacket to him but remembered that he had proposed that they not speak to each other before one o'clock, before each had done their significant work of the day. Then they would have a full lunch.

He vanished from sight into the attached barn and reappeared carrying an enormous maul, a tool Charlotte knew well from when her father used to split wood at their cabin in Minnesota. Nathan set one of the twenty-inch logs on end, stood back, swung the axe over his head, and slammed it into the grain, where it stuck, of course, and resisted his attempts to free it.

She couldn't bear to watch; she supposed he would eventually figure out he needed a wedge, and that splitting thirteen cords of wood might take him the rest of his life. She removed her first attempt at a bowl from the wheel and threw on another clump of clay. A good throw, near the center, and she pressed her hands together, forcing the clay into shape.

Nathan rose at dawn every day and went to work on the woodpile instead of hammering away at his old typewriter. The woodpile became Nathan's new focus. Often she didn't know he had left the bed until she woke to the thud of the maul against an iron wedge. He had also decided to chop in nothing but a long-sleeved underwear shirt and blue jeans. Her breath caught at the sight of his shoulder blades and the knobs of his collarbone. She thought of her father standing in front of the lake in Minnesota on one of their summer visits, spreading his arms like wings and diving into the water.

One day at lunch he asked if she had noticed the kids waiting for the bus down the street. They stood with their hands in their pockets, wearing nothing but T-shirts as steam poured out of their mouths. "It's ten degrees outside, and they're not just pretending not to be cold, they're not *cold,*" he said. He put down his sandwich and immediately set out to acclimatize himself by walking to Boynton's Market in nothing but a V-neck T-shirt. She felt perversely satisfied when he turned right around and immediately plunged himself into a hot bath.

For several days she purposely avoided the firewood, but one morning she went out through the attached barn to the largest of the woodpiles. She saw no sign of Nathan, who had managed, she calculated, to split maybe half a cord, though she supposed he might have fed some of what he'd split into the fire already, supplementing the cord and a half that the previous tenants had left in the basement. She picked up the maul by the neck, tapped a wedge into a split in the grain of one of the big logs, and swung down, hitting the wedge squarely in the middle. You couldn't split cordwood this size with one wedge (especially white oak), and you had to slice at the outer rings before going for the crack in the center. Apparently, Nathan had discovered the same thing, because she found two additional wedges to the left of the pile. When she had split the whole log, she looked up and tasted sweat. Her breath steamed in front of her face, and there stood Nathan in the kitchen window with a cup of coffee just lowered from his lips. He smiled, though not quite with the same satisfaction as when he had seen her outside in bare feet weeks before. She called out to him, asking after the coffee in the pot. At first she thought he hadn't heard, but then he raised a finger in front of his lips. No speaking before one.

The next morning she sat in her studio and listened for the clicking sounds of Nathan's fingers on the keys. Nothing. She had just started to wonder if he'd left his room when his chair scraped back. His slippered feet scuffed across the floors into the kitchen to pause, she thought, in front of the refrigerator or the cupboard.

She packed her clay and this time pushed the heavy wheel itself into the corner of the room, lay down on the pine floor in her thick sweater, crossed her arms over her chest like a person laid to rest, and closed her eyes. She imagined she could hear her father swinging the maul against the wedge, though of course it wasn't her father but Nathan. Her father had always worked at the woodpile in his dark-blue sweatshirt with the hood pulled low over his brow, steam pouring out of the opening for his face as if from the mouth of a cave.

Both she and her mother knew that her father had professional secrets—his job in the military involved training people. They also knew—and she couldn't remember when she first realized this—that he had personal secrets and allowed only part of himself to be known to them.

After her father's death, Charlotte's mother claimed she had known about the other women from the very beginning. "Your father made himself into two people, one he hid from us and showed to others and one he showed just to us," her mother said to her. "You can't tell them you see through them; you can't let on that you know." Charlotte didn't believe her mother at first, but evidence did eventually emerge: her father had a child with another woman in Florida.

Nathan knew her father had died when she was young, but he didn't know the rest of it. If Nathan found out about this part of her life, he'd want to know everything—he'd want more and more until he convinced himself that she had made all of herself visible to him. Only then would he relax. Sometimes she thought Nathan loved her as he did one of his books that had been typed, set, and bound—he didn't want to think there was more to the story.

Charlotte heard a yell from outside, followed by a grumble. Presently Nathan limped through the back door and into the kitchen with blood soaking through a gash in his chinos. He had finally nicked his shin. She rushed to the bathroom for a bandage and peroxide. When she came back, he sat with his elbows on the table, still shaking his head. She pulled up his pant leg and dabbed the bleeding cut with the paper towel.

When she looked up at his unshaven face, his expression startled her. Dark crescents hung under his eyes.

"You don't look so good," she said.

"I haven't been sleeping," he said irritably.

She dabbed at his cut in silence.

"You know, I was thinking about you out there," he said, pursing his lips and nodding his head like a colonel who had just ordered an attack on a hillside stronghold. "I was thinking that if you don't like it here, we can go; we can go back anytime you want."

She pressed the disinfectant against his leg again, making him wince. "We haven't been here that long." She didn't know what on earth she was doing. Her heart had jumped at the idea of leaving this place.

"I know, I know, you're right. Something might come out of me yet, but I think I'm through for good."

"That's what you always say."

"No, I don't—do I? Well, I know you're right, but it doesn't feel . . . I can't get rid of this feeling." He studied her while she pretended not to see him looking and stretched the bandage across his wound.

First with both her parents, and then with each separately, she had gone to the lake in Minnesota every summer for a month. Rolling hills. A cliff rose forty feet above the water. The summer she turned sixteen she met a boy, the son of the man who ran the local store. He stood tall and narrow with pale skin and freckles. David Munro, his long arms paddling the canoe, the tight brown curls of his hair and the way his smile would just appear, like a starling landing on the feeder outside their cabin. He often stuttered in front of her mother, but never with her. When they first started spending time together, he asked about her father. This was years after her parents had split and her father had died. Without meaning to, she told David she had never met her father. Once she lied, she had to keep lying.

On Sundays, when he didn't have to work, David walked all the way around the lake, six miles, to see her, and they hiked through the woods to the cliff. He brought two bottles of soda and cookies taken from the store, and she brought an old blanket. She remembered the coolness of the air in the shade of the forest. When they reached the clearing at the edge of the cliff, there was the touch of his fingers on her naked hip. They went every Sunday to their spot, on a grassy slope high above the lake. She spread the blanket. They took off their clothes—they couldn't wait—and then later, with the sweat drying on their skin, they drank the sodas and went swimming. Usually, they climbed down the trail to the side of the cliff, but the last time they were together before she went back home with her mother, David Munro walked up to the edge of the cliff and dove straight down twenty feet into water so clear she could see all the way to the bottom. His body knifed under, curved through the water, and rose to the surface.

Nathan started rising in the middle of the night, and she heard him pacing downstairs. In the afternoons he went to the library and returned with stacks of books, which he took to his room. One of the books, she saw, was a biography of Benedict Arnold.

At lunch every day he told her about Arnold, who had started off with 1,100 men and marched 350 miles through the middle of the state of Maine in November with hardly any food.

"'They came up the river in bateaux,'" he read aloud. "Ridiculous—these terrible boats made of green pine. They didn't get very far north of Augusta before the boats just started to come apart. It rained, sleeted, snowed; their supplies spoiled; half his men either died or deserted, taking most of the food with them. When the river narrowed, they had to drag what was left of their boats against the current through the freezing water, and when they reached the headwaters, they pushed up the side of the mountains through the woods until their clothes were shredded. They ate bark to survive and dressed in animal skins. When they reached the Saint Lawrence, only six hundred men remained, and they couldn't attack because of sheeting rain—their camp turned into a pool of mud. More of his troops deserted; more died of smallpox. What were they thinking; what drove them on?'"

At first Nathan seemed excited to talk about his reading, but as the week dragged on he grew quieter and on two occasions during their afternoon lunches didn't even answer her questions about his morning. At night, he read by the fire and went to bed, often in his study, without saying a word to her. After lunch one day he walked from room to room inspecting the furniture the owners had left behind. She found him in her studio holding one of the chairs upside down and squinting at the joinery.

"See those tool marks?" he said without looking at her. The sound of his voice startled her. Apparently not interested in an answer, he turned his back to her and leaned toward a large cracked portrait on the interior wall of a man holding a telescope with a ship's rigging in the background. "Do you think this is one of the Howlands?" he said. He leaned toward the canvas. "Those boats in the background are Chinese junks."

She didn't know if she was supposed to answer.

The next afternoon he walked around each room knocking on the plaster with his ear pressed to the wall. She leaned into the front room from the hall and asked him what he was doing. "They hid people in the walls," he said. "That's what the Realtor said. Brought them north on ships, up through the tunnel from the river." He looked at her but didn't seem to see her. Before she could say his name, he continued to the next room, the pine boards creaking under his heels.

They went a week without seeing the sky. When the sun finally appeared one morning through a break in the clouds, even the ground seemed startled by the light. She moved her stool closer to the window of her studio and closed her eyes, feeling the light on her face. Nathan didn't appear in the kitchen at one. She waited 15 minutes and stood by his door. She wasn't supposed to knock when he was in his writing room, no matter what the hour, but she did. He didn't answer, so she forced herself to open the door. Nathan sat at his desk with his head in his hands.

"I have been a good husband," he said.

"Yes?" she said.

"Why don't you just go back to Hastings if it's so hard for you to be here?" he asked.

"What are you talking about? I want to be here." This was a lie, of course, but he couldn't know that.

"I know what you were up to back there in New York," he said quietly. "I've been piecing it together. It must be very hard for you to be away from him."

She felt her stomach sink.

"I should've known this would happen," he said. "I won't say I was waiting for it, but I guess I should've been. I mean, look at me. Can you at least look at me?"

She did, reluctantly. He had deeper circles under his eyes. He'd lost more weight. She started to speak, though she didn't know what would come out. He waved her off. He obviously assumed she was offering an excuse. "I don't understand how you can stand in front of me as if nothing has happened. I see now I must've sensed it, probably the first day you were with him. No wonder you were reluctant to come up here."

"But I was happy to come here. And what do you mean 'him'? Who? Nathan, you're being ridiculous," she said, her voice hysterical in her own ears. Most of her friends were women, except for Henry, who was gay.

"Yes, who?" he said calmly, looking at the floor. "That's the question."

There seemed no point in trying to defend herself when there was nothing to defend. She took a deep breath and tried to remember that he sometimes worked himself up over small things. He gazed around his writing room. With a shake of his head, he got up, walked past her.

She pulled on her jacket with shaking hands and went out to the driveway, where she immediately felt the bite of the air on her cheeks. Tears streamed down her face and dripped over her chin into her mittens. *Cliché,* Nathan would think if he was here.

Charlotte wrapped her arms around her chest and looked down the hill. The river looked frozen solid between frosted banks, though she was sure a current still flowed under the ice.

The summer she turned twelve her father took her alone up to their lake camp. He had fought with her mother the whole previous year, and Charlotte thought they might get divorced. The night they arrived, he started talking about grace and dignity as they sat in front of the fireplace. There were two kinds of grace: the kind that came to you free and the kind you had to put together from scratch. He had no respect for the former, just as he had no respect for the kind of dignity acquired without great difficulty.

In the kitchen Nathan sat hunched over his dinner and didn't look up when she shut the door behind her and stood above him. She said his name in a voice calculated to avoid the kind of hysterics he abhorred, especially in other people's fiction. But he didn't answer; he had finally stopped talking to her. After a while, he slid back his chair with exaggerated composure and took his plate upstairs.

Several days passed and she found herself standing in her studio staring down at her wheel and bag of clay and trying to recall the person who had once been interested in forming pots. That person—her for eight years now—seemed to have vanished as if she'd never existed. She closed her eyes and listened. The noon whistle echoed down the valley from the firehouse, the faint vibration passing into her fingers minutes before the train passed through, and she heard the sound of trucks driving up the street. The door slammed when Nathan returned from his walk.

Now she could begin her own walk without fear of running into him. She set out with a brisk pace past the old houses, most of them fixed up but some sagging and clad with asbestos. Last winter's road sand crunched under her heels. Snow began to fall, obscuring her view of the river. She was on a march, she realized—Arnold's march against the miles standing between him and the English. She hadn't gone more than a mile, leaning her head into the wind that funneled down the valley, when she pulled up short with the feeling that someone was watching her. She turned around several times to make sure and once even waited behind a tree to see if anyone would appear, but no one did.

On Sunday, she approached the mute door of Nathan's room. In the many moments that she had stopped outside his door over the years she had learned to detect his moods from the force of a page ruffling or the tempo and rhythm of the keys. If only the typewriter would start snapping again, they could go back to their lives. She pounded her fist on the panel so hard she thought at first the whole doorframe might collapse.

"Come out of there!" she yelled. "I can't just sit here by myself with no one to talk to."

He appeared in the doorway, calm and contained. The sight of his Oxford tucked into his khakis and his salt-and-pepper hair made her feel disheveled and slightly crazy.

"You have no idea what this feels like, do you?" he said.

"Nathan, I have no idea what you're talking about." She tried to control her voice.

"I can't think. I can't work. It's not the physical part of it that upsets me. It's that you love him."

"But I'm in love with *you*," she said helplessly.

"You saw me from across the room that night at my reading. You were telling yourself a story about me instead of listening to the story I was reading. And now you don't like what you see. I knew you would take everything from me." He shook his head and closed the door.

She woke in the morning and couldn't seem to get out of bed. She was hungry, but she couldn't eat. A fever boiled up through her legs, blushing the skin of her belly until she broke out in a cold sweat. The winter light cut at the back of her eyes. She began to sense someone lingering at the edge of her thoughts, drawing her back into sleep. Then he was in the room with her, standing over her bed. She couldn't see his face at first but could sense his presence. He drew so close to her that his features were clear in every detail, his thin nose and pale, almost translucent skin. Convinced that the man Nathan accused her of loving had appeared to her, she rushed downstairs and searched through the kitchen drawers for a pad of paper and a pencil to draw him, but by the time she sat down at the table and leaned forward, her hand shaking, he had vanished. Her stomach squeezed the air out of her lungs. She loved this other man, just as Nathan had said, and she couldn't live without the smell of his skin and the touch of his hand, sensations she somehow knew exactly but had never experienced. The tip of the pencil rested on the lined paper, leaving nothing but a small gray dot. She knew the feeling but not the sound of the man's voice. She had seen his face but couldn't picture it.

She lay in bed, and by evening, when her fever started to break, the man reappeared in her thoughts, walking slowly down a street away from her. He had short gray hair. She couldn't catch up. When she saw him one last time, before dawn, he sat on the other side of the frozen river, looking across at her, three hundred yards of ice between them.

The understanding that the man had left for good spread like blue ink through her thoughts. The sun rose above the hill on the opposite side of the valley, filling her room with a sheer white light. Another day. How long had she been in bed? She fell back asleep and woke sometime in the afternoon. Starving, she went down to the kitchen, poured a glass of milk, and drank in gulps until her stomach unclenched. She cracked six eggs and dropped them in the iron skillet with a hunk of cheddar. Stuffing one piece of bread in her mouth with a slice of butter, she cut up the rest and tossed the slices on the grate in the oven. The heat from the stove rushed over her face as the pepper, crackling with the eggs, stung her nose. She ate everything.

Nathan came into the kitchen, and she tried not to notice his ashen cheeks, his bony shoulders under his frayed button-down. He sat opposite her at the table and rested his forehead in his palm. The low sun moved to the west, casting the kitchen in gloom. When he reached out and took her hand, he squeezed so hard that the knuckles of her fingers pinched together.

"I am so sorry. I don't know what's been wrong with me. Can you forgive me?" he said, his voice faltering. He sounded like a boy. "I don't know what happened."

For several moments she looked at the side of his head and felt empty. Still hungry. She thought of telling him that he need not worry, that he struggled with his writing. But she couldn't. She saw no way forward.

"There are things I haven't told you," she said, as surprised by her words as he must have been. His eyes widened, and his hand pulled off the table and into his lap. Desperate, suddenly, to hold his attention, she leaned closer to him. "When I was young," she said, "my father and I went to our cabin on a lake in Minnesota." She described the size of the lake and the color of the sky in the summer, the pine smell of their cabin, the old metal Grumman canoe they pulled up on the beach. She told him about the village on the opposite side of the lake, smaller than Vaughn, a ghost town except in the summer.

"Where was your mother?" Nathan asked, his brow furrowing.

"It was just the two of us the summer after my parents split," she said, knowing she had to talk fast. "We were there for five weeks that summer, five long weeks in the rain with nothing to do." She told Nathan about going out in the canoe with her father to fish and how he would just lie there in the bottom of the boat or sit on the seat with his head in his hands, and how back in the cabin they had little food. And he wouldn't speak; he sat at the table, fed the woodstove, and drank Scotch.

"I want you to know this," she said. "He wasn't violent." Which was true. He'd never raised his voice, not once that she could remember. "But I was afraid of him," she said, and this was true as well. "One night," she continued, not knowing what she would say next but looking Nathan right in the eyes, "he waited for me to go to bed, and he sat there in the main room. He took out his revolver." She felt Nathan's breath on her lashes. "After I turned out the light in my bedroom, he put the barrel in his mouth and held it there. I don't know how long. I waited for it to go off, but it didn't, and then he took the gun out of his mouth. He did the same thing the next night," she said, "and the next."

She held her voice steady by tightening her grip on Nathan's hand. "You have to understand . . ." Her voice rose as she lifted her chin into the air. Nathan nodded quickly, impatiently, afraid, it seemed, that she wouldn't go on. "I started to feel that whatever was going on in him was also going on in me. One night after he fell asleep in the chair, I walked into the living room, picked the gun off his lap, and I shot him in the head."

Nathan's eyes froze. The vein in his temple pounded, and she continued with what happened next: she set the gun near his hand, and she stood in the room until light filled the air outside the windows. No close neighbors, and every direction she could think of running led nowhere. She started walking through the woods and down the dirt road. Her footsteps accompanied the rain pattering through the maples. Six miles to the town on the other side of the lake, and as she walked down the corridor of pines, some part of her thought her father might drive around the corner. Maybe he'd been shopping, to buy a new fishing rod, lumber, or food. He would drive up alongside her and push open the passenger door and tell her to hop inside. From the town, she called her mother, who drove across the state to pick her up. Together they walked into the cabin to find what was there.

Nathan looked away for a moment, shook his head, and looked back at her. She saw her reflection in his pupils. He tried to flush her away with tears, but he blinked and she was there again. He couldn't believe, he said, that she had kept this from him for all these years. Even though she still felt hungry, she took Nathan by the hand and led him up the stairs to the bedroom. The air was freezing, but her skin was hot. He climbed slowly and wouldn't let go of her hand. He said he hadn't slept in days. She undressed him as he stood in the dark with his arms at his side, and they lay next to each other under the comforter.

Within moments Nathan fell sound asleep, his hand cradled against her chest and his mouth slack against the pillow. The winter moon covered him with silver light, revealing what he would look like in twenty years, an old man, washed of all color like a weathered bone.

She propped herself on one elbow and gazed through the window and down the hill to the dark colonial houses on Second Street. The town was asleep except for the streetlamps stationed every half block like sentries. Without waking, Nathan stirred and grabbed for her hand as if afraid she wouldn't be there. She was here, though, wide awake, vigilant.

"It's awful," he whispered. "It's an awful story." He was so tired that he sounded drunk. She put her hand over his lips and saw as he closed his lids that her story would play over and over in his thoughts until he believed her. He needed a story he could believe. They both did. When they woke in the morning, they would pack the car and head east along the river and south toward home. He wouldn't ask her a single question—she wouldn't have to say another word.

Sarah Campbell's Story

(1741)

Sarah Campbell Howland,
Ada Campbell

*In 1803 Sarah Campbell Howland told her story to her grand-
daughter, Emma Howland, who wrote the story down and,
shortly before she died, passed it to her granddaughter, Elizabeth
Carlton.*

My grandmother Sarah Campbell was born in Port Ellen on
the Isle of Islay, Scotland on August 13, 1722, to pious parents who
instructed her in the Christian religion. When she was about nine-
teen years old, her father went to Pennsylvania, and finding land
suitable for his family, he wrote for her mother and the children
to take passage in the first vessel and come to Pennsylvania. Her
mother, with three daughters, left on board a large ship. On July
28, 1741, they sailed from Glasgow, Captain Knight commander.

For some time after they sailed, they had pleasant weather, and everything was agreeable, excepting their seasickness. The ship's company daily assembled on the quarterdeck for prayers, which were performed alternately by four or five of the passengers, to the great satisfaction of many on board.

When they had been about three weeks at sea, a mortal fever broke out and spread through the ship's company. Not one was able to help another. Sarah's mother and her children were preserved and restored to health, though many died around them.

After ten weeks at sea, they were visited with a violent storm. Waves rose above the mast, and a ceiling of water blew from peak to peak above them. Their ship was damaged, and they were all very near being lost. The captain said they were close to land and expected every day to make it. But the violence of the storm drove them to eastward. Their masts gave way, and they were in a distressed situation.

At that time the captain thought proper to put all hands on allowance, as he did not know where the ship was, or how long they should be continued in their present situation. He knew not where to steer his course. One biscuit a day, a small portion of meat, and a quart of water was all their allowance. This was continued for ten or twelve days, and then they were put upon half allowance, excepting the water, which was continued the same. Then days after, they spoke a ship, which supplied them with provisions, but their allowance was not increased.

October 28 they made land on the eastern coast, and found it to be a desolate island a mile from shore, inhabited only by a few Indians, called Seguin. The ship was anchored, and they remained a few days on board. The captain and others took the longboat and went hoping to find some French inhabitants but returned without success. The passengers were then ordered to land. Many boatloads of people were scattered round the island, without any food. The number of people could not be less than a hundred. They were told that the last boats would bring them provisions, but were disappointed. Nothing was sent to the island. Some cried, some almost distracted, not knowing what to do.

Sarah and her family were landed in one of the first boats. Her youngest sister died in the boat, but she, her older sister, and their mother reached the shore. All being in confusion and trouble, there was no one to bury the girl. When the boats were landing, as she stood on the beach, a child, about two years old, was put into Sarah's arms. She looked around to see who was to take it from her, but found no one that would own it. Sarah inquired, who takes care of this child? A little boy, about twelve years old, answered, Nobody, ma'am, but I. How she felt, knowing that this child's parents had both died in the ship. Sarah was obliged to lay down the child and leave it to the care of Him who had the care of them all. The boy and the child were soon after found dead, lying together.

Twenty or thirty of the passengers set out to look for inhabitants, but were never after heard of again. The captain, mate, and seamen left the ship and went in search of inhabitants. After a few days' sail eastward, they fell in with land, and came to a place called New Harbor, about thirty miles east of the Kennebec River. Getting two small vessels there, they came back for the plunder of the ship, which had been cast upon the rocks and broken to pieces. They collected what plunder they could and returned to New Harbor, taking with them a handful of people from the island. These were sold for their passage, but in this way delivered from this distressing situation. The rest of the passengers were left on the island.

Sarah and her sister found some mussels on the beach, which with sea-kelp and dulse they boiled in a pot they had brought on shore. This was the only food they had. God supported them even at that time, and gave Sarah hope of relief, which she ever maintained in the very darkest hour. Every day, more died around them. It was observed that the men failed sooner than the women. There was scarcely one to help another, as everyone had sufficient to do for himself. The provision for the day was to be sought in the day.

The Indians soon visited them, and added much to their distress, robbing them of everything they had brought from the ship. In a severe snowstorm, they hung their clothes on trees as shelter. The Indians came and took them for themselves. When Sarah tried to resist them, one drew his hatchet and attempted to strike her. She drew back and let them take what they pleased. Among other things, they took their pot, in which they boiled their mussels. This was only a few years before King George's War led to more fighting with the French and Indians in all the eastern settlements.

Sarah went to see a friend, who lay at a little distance, in a feeble state, unable to rise. She asked the friend whether she had anything to eat. She said, yes, her shipmates had given her mussels when they got any for themselves, but added she could eat some boiled dulse, if she could get any. Sarah said she would get her some tomorrow. On the morrow, returning to see her, Sarah found her dead, and several more by her. Walking along the shore, she found a boy, about seventeen years old, sitting very disconsolate, with a book in his hand. Sarah asked him, What do you do here? He answered, I am looking for the captain, who is coming to carry me off the island. Sarah said to him, Did he promise you that favor? Yes, he said. Well, Sarah replied, don't depend on it. He wept bitterly, but Sarah could not persuade him to give up hope. In a few days she found him dead with his Bible open under his head.

The people began to die now very fast. There was no traveling anywhere but dead bodies were found, as few were buried. All were so weak and helpless that they had enough to do to keep life in themselves. In this distressing situation, Sarah, her sister Ada, and her mother remained until every person, of whom they had knowledge on the island, was dead.

Their fire went out, and they had nothing to strike with. Several snows had fallen, but soon melted. Another snow fell when they were in such distress. They had nothing to cover themselves but the heavens and nothing to eat but frozen mussels. Their mother died, a lifeless corpse by their side. They were not able to bury her or do anything with her. Sarah's sister Ada began to fail very fast, and her spirits were very low. They lay down next to some trees to rest their heads. Soon Sarah rose and went down to the beach, for some frozen mussels, and carried them to her sister, who ate them. Now their courage began to falter. They saw nothing to expect but death, yet did not wholly give up their hope of deliverance. There they were, two distressed sisters surrounded by dead bodies, without food or fire, and almost without clothing. Sarah had no shoes to her feet, which were much swollen by the cold. The ground was covered with snow, and the season was fast advancing, it being nearly the middle of December, so that they had every reason to expect that they should soon share the fate of their companions.

To their great surprise, they saw three men on the island, who, when they approached, appeared no less surprised to find them living. Sarah took courage and spoke to them of their distress. The men appeared pitiful, told them that they had come from New Harbor with two vessels for plunder, and offered to take them on board. Sarah and her sister complied with their invitation and were ferried to the vessel. As she was rising from the frozen ground, by the assistance of one of the men, she put out her hand to take a small bundle, which she had preserved through all their difficulties, and which contained some clothes and books, especially her Bible. Seeing her attempt to take it, the men promised to take care of it for her. Trusting to their honor, she left it with them, but she never saw it again.

After they were on board, the men treated them kindly. The captain gave each of them a spoonful of spirit and half a biscuit. This was the first bread they had tasted for two months. When collecting the plunder, the men told them they should have whatever they claimed as belonging to them. This was more than they expected. After plundering the ship and stripping the dead, they sailed. Then she saw the last of the terrible place. In a short time, they arrived in New Harbor. Their new friends then announced plans to sell them as servants to satisfy themselves for their trouble in saving their lives. This was a trial most insupportable.

But to their great comfort, a man came on board, who was from the same place in Scotland from which they had come. He was kind and pitiful, and endeavored to comfort them. He took them to his house, and there bid them to be of good cheer, for he would not suffer such rough men to take advantage of them. This gentleman gave them every consolation in his power, and conversed with them in a very Christian manner, which was affecting and comforting.

They tarried with him until they had so far recovered as to be able to work for their living. The gentleman wrote to their father in Pennsylvania, informing him of the situation, and did all he could to forward the letter as soon as possible. This was about the last of December 1741. In the meantime he provided good places for them. Sarah's sister was sent to live with a friend of his, at Boothbay, and was very happily situated. Soon after she went there, a revival of religion took place among the people. Sarah tarried at New Harbor through the winter. The next spring she came to where we live now, in the Sheepscot Bay, and was employed in a family on Georgetown Island. There she enjoyed the privileges of religion as well as very kind treatment. Both the man and his wife were teachers and were greatly animated by the good work that was going on in the place. At the time, there was manifest a general attention to religion. Having no minister, the people met together every Sabbath, and frequently on other days, for the purpose of worshipping God in the public manner.

Sarah had an offer of marriage from a man named Robert Howland, who lived on nearby Howland Island, and her situation seemed to urge her to accept. She lived very happily with her husband for thirty years, and they had eight children, two sons and six daughters. The name of the ship that left Glasgow for America was called *Grand Design*. Sarah and her sister survived sixty days on Seguin Island.

About the Author

Jason Brown grew up in Maine. He was a Stegner Fellow and Truman Capote Fellow at Stanford and now teaches in the MFA program at the University of Oregon. His short stories have appeared in *The Atlantic, Harper's, Best American Short Stories, The Pushcart Prize Anthology, NPR's Selected Shorts, The Missouri Review*, and other places. He has published two story collections, *Driving the Heart* (1999) and *Why the Devil Chose New England for His Work* (2007).

Acknowledgements

I would like to thank the people who made this book possible: Kristine and Speer and the people at *The Missouri Review*, Nicola and Isabel Fucigna, Julie Barer, George Smith, Keith Scribner, Frank Burroughs, Marjorie Celona, Willing Davidson, my stepfather Bill Caldwell for the tale on which "Sarah Campbell's Story" is based, Colin Sargent and the people at *Portland Monthly*, and the editors at reviews who took a chance on these stories.